CZECH FOLK TALES

CZECH FOLK TALES

SELECTED AND TRANSLATED BY

DR. JOSEF BAUDIS, M.R.I.A.

LECTURER IN COMPARATIVE PHILOLOGY
AT THE PRAGUE UNIVERSITY

WITH 8 ILLUSTRATIONS

LONDON: GEORGE ALLEN & UNWIN LTD.
RUSKIN HOUSE   40 MUSEUM STREET, W.C. 1

PREFACE

THE present collection has been selected from the following sources :—

Josef Kubín, Povídky kladské, i., ii. (in " Národopisný věstník českoslovanský ").

V. Vondrák, Několik pohádek z Dubu u Vodňan (S. Bohemia), in " Český Lid," xiii.

V. Tille, Povídky sebrané na Valašsku (S. Moravia). " Národopisný sborník českoslovanský," Svazek vii. Prague, 1901.

Elpl, Řada pohádek a pověstí nasbíraných v Líšni u Brna (Moravia).

B. M. Kulda, Moravské národní pohádky a pověsti, i. (Prague, 1874). From Moravia.

The first two stories (" Twelve Months," " Vítazko ") have been retold by the novelist Božena Němcová (from the Slovak).

My translation could not be, of course, a literal one, because many phrases in the original might seem strange to the English reader's ear.

Finally, I wish to express my thanks to Miss Eleanor Hull and Mr. Robin Flower for revising my English.

JOSEF BAUDIŠ.

LONDON, *October* 1917.

CONTENTS

xi

The first two illustrations are copies of pictures by Joseph Manes; the others have been drawn by Mr. E. Staněk, who in some cases has adapted drawings by Mikuláš Aleš.

INTRODUCTION

THE present collection is intended to exemplify the spirit of the Czech race. It may perhaps be objected that folk-tale themes are part of a common stock belonging to all European races, and even to many primitive peoples: but though this is perfectly true, it is also no less certain that the spirit of the nation manifests itself in the manner of their telling. The selection has been made from all sorts of folk tales, artistic and primitive alike ; and yet two things are common to all of them : the moral tendency and a sense of humour. By this I do not mean morality in the vulgar sense of retribution for evil, or of filial devotion, or the sentimental insistence upon " every one living happily ever afterwards," and above all upon Jack marrying his Molly. I mean that higher sort of morality which was the mainspring of Protestantism. It is often supposed that Protestantism is very unfavourable to the development and preservation of folk tales; but those of Bohemia are certainly an exception to this rule. The Czech nation was the first to adopt the Protestant faith, and even to-day is still Protestant at heart, though the Habsburgs forced it back into the Catholic fold.

The Czechs, then, have preserved their love for folk tales, adapting them to the higher morality and to the national sentiment, and discarding many of their supernatural features, or where the supernatural was allowed to remain for a moment, reverting very soon to the strict limits of probability. It is the very same method which, for example, Mr. Wells employs in some of his novels. That the Slav nations have a certain tendency to lay stress upon the ethical side in their folk tales has already been pointed out by the Czech poet Erben, whose tales have been translated into English in Wratislaw's Collection.

As for their humour, the Czechs have a natural tendency to satire. The best works in Old Czech literature are satires, and in modern times one of the most brilliant of Czech politicians, Karel Havliček, was also the greatest Czech satirist. This spirit may also be seen in the present collection ; but in every case the story-teller, instead of assuming the attitude of the morality preacher or of indulging in theatrical invective against the wickedness of the times, rests content with a good-humoured gibe at the folly of the world, at the frailty of his fellow-men, and, it may be, at his own.

These two traits are inherent in the nature of the Czech people ; and those who know their love of such tales and of the literature which has grown out of them, can realize their search for a haven of refuge from the cruel present and their fond dream-pictures of a land where all was good, where at last everything was bound to end well, where truth and justice at last had conquered. Alas! to the victims of Habsburg rule and Austrian bayonets the bare possibility seemed utterly excluded. And yet why should they not dream of such a land? *Amo quia absurdum !* But at the very moment their humorous *ego* could not suppress a sneer. Yes, even in that wonderland which their fancy painted are foolish kings, ever prone to break their word : even there people are bad and stupid ! But our tale says that the bad were vanquished and the foolish put to shame : let, then, the tale be told ! And even as he tells it, his heart nurses the inward hope that the foreign tyrants who oppress him may one day be vanquished and annihilated.

That such were the wishes of the Czech people, the Great War has shown. They have proved by their deeds their love of freedom ; and to-day Czechs are fighting bravely in every Allied army and in their own national units formed in Russia. May their Austrian oppressors be brought to the ground, and may Bohemia regain the freedom for which she has longed for three centuries !

THE TWELVE MONTHS

ONCE upon a time there lived a mother who had two daughters. One was her own child, the other her stepdaughter. She was very fond of her own daughter, but she would not so much as look at her stepdaughter. The only reason was that Maruša, the stepdaughter, was prettier than her own daughter, Holena. The gentle-hearted Maruša did not know how beautiful she was, and so she could never make out why her mother was so cross with her whenever she looked at her. She had to do all the housework, tidying up the cottage, cooking, washing, and sewing, and then she had to take the hay to the cow and look after her. She did all this work alone, while Holena spent the time adorning herself and lazing about. But Maruša liked work, for she was a patient girl, and when her mother scolded and rated her, she bore it like a lamb. It was no

1

good, however, for they grew crueller and crueller every day, only because Maruša was growing prettier and Holena uglier every day.

At last the mother thought : " Why should I keep a pretty stepdaughter in my house? When the lads come courting here, they will fall in love with Maruša and they won't look at Holena."

From that moment the stepmother and her daughter were constantly scheming how to get rid of poor Maruša. They starved her and they beat her. But she bore it all, and in spite of all she kept on growing prettier every day. They invented torments that the cruellest of men would never have thought of.

One day—it was in the middle of January— Holena felt a longing for the scent of violets.

" Go, Maruša, and get me some violets from the forest ; I want to wear them at my waist and to smell them," she said to her sister.

" Great heavens ! sister. What a strange notion ! Who ever heard of violets growing under the snow?" said poor Maruša.

" You wretched tatterdemalion ! how dare you argue when I tell you to do something ? Off you go at once, and if you don't bring me violets from the forest I'll kill you!" said Holena threateningly.

The stepmother caught hold of Maruša, turned her out of the door, and slammed it to after her. She went into the forest weeping bitterly. The snow lay deep, and there wasn't a human footprint to be seen. Maruša wandered about for a long time, tortured by hunger and trembling with cold. She begged God to take her from the world.

At last she saw a light in the distance. She went towards the glow, and came at last to the top of a mountain. A big fire was burning there, and round the fire were twelve stones with twelve men sitting on them. Three of them had snow-white beards, three were not so old, and three were still younger. The three youngest were the handsomest of them all. They were not speaking, but all sitting silent. These twelve men were the twelve months. Great January sat highest of all; his hair and beard were as white as snow, and in his hand he held a club.

Maruša was frightened. She stood still for a time in terror, but, growing bolder, she went up to them and said: " Please, kind

sirs, let me warm my hands at your fire.   I
am trembling with the cold."

Great January nodded, and asked her :
"Why have you come here, my dear little
girl?   What are you looking for?"

"I am looking for violets," answered
Maruša.

"This is no time to be looking for violets,
for everything is covered with snow," answered
Great January.

"Yes, I know ; but my sister Holena and
my stepmother said that I must bring them
some violets from the forest.   If I don't
bring them, they'll kill me.   Tell me, fathers,
please tell me where I can find them."

Great January stood up and went to one
of the younger months—it was March—and,
giving him the club, he said : "Brother, take
the high seat."

March took the high seat upon the stone
and waved the club over the fire.   The fire
blazed up, the snow began to melt, the trees
began to bud, and the ground under the
young beech-trees was at once covered with
grass and the crimson daisy buds began to
peep through the grass.   It was springtime.
Under the bushes the violets were blooming

among their little leaves, and before Maruša had time to think, so many of them had sprung up that they looked like a blue cloth spread out on the ground.

" Pick them quickly, Maruša ! " commanded March.

Maruša picked them joyfully till she had a big bunch. Then she thanked the months with all her heart and scampered merrily home.

Holena and the stepmother wondered when they saw Maruša bringing the violets. They opened the door to her, and the scent of violets filled all the cottage.

"Where did you get them ? " asked Holena sulkily.

" They are growing under the bushes in a forest on the high mountains."

Holena put them in her waistband. She let her mother smell them, but she did not say to her sister : "Smell them."

Another day she was lolling near the stove, and now she longed for some strawberries. So she called to her sister and said : "Go, Maruša, and get me some strawberries from the forest."

"Alas! dear sister, where could I find any

strawberries? Who ever heard of strawberries growing under the snow?" said Maruša.

"You wretched little tatterdemalion, how dare you argue when I tell you to do a thing? Go at once and get me the strawberries, or I'll kill you!"

The stepmother caught hold of Maruša and pushed her out of the door and shut it after her. Maruša went to the forest weeping bitterly. The snow was lying deep, and there wasn't a human footprint to be seen anywhere. She wandered about for a long time, tortured by hunger and trembling with cold. At last she saw the light she had seen the other day. Overjoyed, she went towards it. She came to the great fire with the twelve months sitting round it.

"Please, kind sirs, let me warm my hands at the fire. I am trembling with cold."

Great January nodded, and asked her: "Why have you come again, and what are you looking for here?"

"I am looking for strawberries."

"But it is winter now, and strawberries don't grow on the snow," said January.

"Yes, I know," said Maruša sadly; "but my sister Holena and my stepmother bade me bring them some strawberries, and if I don't bring them, they will kill me. Tell me, fathers, tell me, please, where I can find them."

Great January arose. He went over to the month sitting opposite to him—it was June—and handed the club to him, saying: "Brother, take the high seat."

June took the high seat upon the stone and swung the club over the fire. The fire shot up, and its heat melted the snow in a moment. The ground was all green, the trees were covered with leaves, the birds began to sing, and the forest was filled with all kinds of flowers. It was summer. The ground under the bushes was covered with white starlets, the starry blossoms were turning into strawberries every minute. They ripened at once, and before Maruša had time to think, there were so many of them that it looked as though blood had been sprinkled on the ground.

"Pick them at once, Maruša!" commanded June.

Maruša picked them joyfully till she had filled her apron full. Then she thanked the months with all her heart and scampered merrily home. Holena and the stepmother wondered when they saw Maruša bringing the strawberries. Her apron was full of them. They ran to open the door for her, and the scent of the strawberries filled the whole cottage.

"Where did you pick them?" asked Holena sulkily.

"There are plenty of them growing under the young beech-trees in the forest on the high mountains."

Holena took the strawberries, and went on eating them till she could eat no more. So did the stepmother too, but they didn't say to Maruša : " Here is one for you."

When Holena had enjoyed the strawberries, she grew greedy for other dainties, and so on the third day she longed for some red apples.

"Maruša, go into the forest and get me some red apples," she said to her sister.

"Alas ! sister dear, how am I to get apples for you in winter?" protested Maruša.

"You wretched little tatterdemalion, how dare you argue when I tell you to do a thing? Go to the forest at once, and if you don't bring me the apples I will kill you!" threatened Holena.

The stepmother caught hold of Maruša and pushed her out of the door and shut it after her. Maruša went to the forest weeping bitterly. The snow was lying deep; there wasn't a human footprint to be seen anywhere. But she didn't wander about this time. She ran straight to the top of the mountain where the big fire was burning. The twelve months were sitting round the fire; yes, there they certainly were, and Great January was sitting on the high seat.

"Please, kind sirs, let me warm my hands at the fire. I am trembling with cold."

Great January nodded, and asked her: "Why have you come here, and what are you looking for?"

"I am looking for red apples."

"It is winter now, and red apples don't grow in winter," answered January.

"Yes, I know," said Maruša sadly; "but my sister and my stepmother, too, bade me bring them some red apples from the forest. If I don't bring them, they will kill me. Tell me, father, tell me, please, where I could find them."

Great January rose up. He went over to

one of the older months—it was September. He handed the club to him and said: "Brother, take the high seat."

Month September took the high seat upon the stone and swung the club over the fire. The fire began to burn with a red flame, the snow began to melt. But the trees were not covered with leaves; the leaves were wavering down one after the other, and the cold wind was driving them to and fro over the yellowing ground. This time Maruša did not see so many flowers. Only red pinks were blooming on the hillside, and meadow saffrons were flowering in the valley. High fern and thick ivy were growing under the young beech-trees. But Maruša was only looking for red apples, and at last she saw an apple-tree with red apples hanging high among its branches.

"Shake the tree at once, Maruša!" commanded the month.

Right gladly Maruša shook the tree, and one apple fell down. She shook it a second time, and another apple fell down.

"Now, Maruša, run home quickly!" shouted the month.

Maruša obeyed at once. She picked up

the apples, thanked the months with all her heart, and ran merrily home.

Holena and the stepmother wondered when they saw Maruša bringing the apples. They ran to open the door for her, and she gave them two apples.

"Where did you get them?" asked Holena.

"There are plenty of them in the forest on the high mountain."

"And why didn't you bring more? Or did you eat them on the way home?" said Holena harshly.

"Alas! sister dear, I didn't eat a single one. But when I had shaken the tree once, one apple fell down, and when I shook it a second time, another apple fell down, and they wouldn't let me shake it again. They shouted to me to go straight home," protested Maruša.

Holena began to curse her: "May you be struck to death by lightning!" and she was going to beat her.

Maruša began to cry bitterly, and she prayed to God to take her to Himself, or she would be killed by her wicked sister and her stepmother. She ran away into the kitchen.

Greedy Holena stopped cursing and began

to eat the apple. It tasted so delicious that she told her mother she had never tasted anything so nice in all her life. The step-mother liked it too. When they had finished, they wanted some more.

" Mother, give me my fur coat. I'll go to the forest myself. That ragged little wretch would eat them all up again on her way home. I'll find the place all right, and I'll shake them all down, however they shout at me."

Her mother tried to dissuade her, but it was no good. She took her fur coat, wrapped a cloth round her head, and off she went to the forest. Her mother stood on the threshold, watching to see how Holena would manage to walk in the wintry weather.

The snow lay deep, and there wasn't a human footprint to be seen anywhere. Holena wandered about for a long time, but the desire of the sweet apple kept driving her on. At last she saw a light in the distance. She went towards it, and climbed to the top of the mountain where the big fire was burning, and round the fire on twelve stones the twelve months were sitting. She was terrified at first, but she soon recovered. She stepped up to the fire and stretched out her hands to warm them, but she didn't say as much as " By your leave " to the twelve months ; no, she didn't say a single word to them.

" Why have you come here, and what are you looking for ? " asked Great January crossly.

" Why do you want to know, you old fool ? It's no business of yours," replied Holena angrily, and she turned away from the fire and went into the forest.

Great January frowned and swung the club over his head. The sky grew dark in a moment, the fire burned low, the snow began to fall as thick as if the feathers had been shaken out of a down quilt, and an icy wind began to blow through the forest. Holena couldn't see one step in front of her ; she lost her way altogether, and several times she fell into snowdrifts. Then her limbs grew weak and began slowly to stiffen. The snow kept on falling and the icy wind blew more icily than ever. Holena began to curse Maruša and the Lord God. Her limbs began to freeze, despite her fur coat.

Her mother was waiting for Holena; she kept on looking out for her, first at the window, then outside the door, but all in vain.

"Does she like the apples so much that she can't leave them, or what is the matter? I must see for myself where she is," decided the stepmother at last. So she put on her fur coat, she wrapped a shawl round her head, and went out to look for Holena. The snow was lying deep; there wasn't a human footprint to be seen; the snow fell fast, and the icy wind was blowing through the forest.

Maruša had cooked the dinner, she had seen to the cow, and yet Holena and her mother did not come back. "Where are they staying so long?" thought Maruša, as she sat down to work at the distaff. The spindle was full already and it was quite dark in the room, and yet Holena and the stepmother had not come back.

"Alas, Lord! what has come to them?" cried Maruša, peering anxiously through the window. The sky was bright and the earth was all glittering, but there wasn't a human soul to be seen. . . . Sadly she shut the window ; she crossed herself, and prayed for her sister and her mother. . . . In the morning she waited with breakfast, she waited with dinner ; but however much she waited, it was no good. Neither her mother nor her sister ever came back. Both of them were frozen to death in the forest.

So good Maruša inherited the cottage, a piece of ploughland and the cow. She married a kind husband, and they both lived happily ever after.

VÍŤAZKO

ONCE there was a mother, and, being a mother, she had a son. She suckled him for twice seven years. After that she took him into a forest and told him to pull up a fir-tree, roots and all. But the lad could not pull up the fir-tree.

"You are not strong enough yet," said the mother. So she suckled him for another seven years. When she had suckled him for thrice seven years, she took him to the forest again and told him to pull up a beech-tree, roots and all. He seized hold of the beech and pulled it up.

"Now you are strong enough. So you are Victor (Víťazko). Now you can provide for me."

"Yes, I will. Only tell me what I can do for you."

"You must get me a good house first, and then you can take me there," said the mother, and she went home.

Víťazko took the beech-tree which he had
pulled up, and, carrying it in his hand like
a club, he started in search of a house for
his mother. Following the wind, he walked
by old roads and paths until he came to a
castle. This castle was inhabited by griffins.

When Víťazko reached the castle, the
griffins would not let him in. But he did
not wait long for their permission : he smashed
the gate and went into the castle and killed
the griffins; their bodies he flung over the
wall, and then he went for a walk through
the castle. He was pleased with everything
he saw. The rooms were nice, nine in
number, but the tenth was closed. When he
had gone through the nine he went into the
tenth, and there he saw a griffin chained to
the wall by three iron bands.

"What are you doing here?" asked
Víťazko.

"I am sitting here, as you see. My
brothers have chained me here. Untie my
bonds and I will give you a splendid reward."

"You must be a wicked old rascal if your
own brothers tied you there. I won't un-
fasten your bonds either," said Víťazko.

So he slammed the door, and went off to

fetch his mother to the castle. When he had brought her there, he showed her everything, but he did not open the tenth room, and he forbade her to enter that room, for otherwise there would be trouble. As soon as Vítazko left the house, the mother could not rest, and she kept on walking near the door of that tenth room, till at last she went in, and, of course, she found the griffin there.

"What are you doing here, and who are you?"

"I am a griffin. My own brothers chained me here. They would have unfastened my bonds again, but your son has killed them all. Untie my bonds and I will reward you, and, if you like, I will marry you," said the griffin.

"And what would Vítazko say?" answered the mother.

"What could he say? We will put him out of the world, and you will be your own mistress."

The mother hesitated long enough, but at last she consented, and then she asked the griffin how she could untie his bonds.

"Go into the cellar and fetch me a cup of wine from the last cask."

The mother went into the cellar and brought him a glass of wine from the last cask. As soon as he had drained the first cup, crash! the first chain fell down. The mother brought him another cup and—well! the second chain snapped. So he begged her to bring him a third cup, and when she brought him the third cup the third chain broke too and the griffin was free again.

"But what am I to tell my son when he comes back?" said the mother anxiously.

"Oh! you must feign illness, and when he asks you what will save you, say that nothing can save you but a suckling of the earth sow. When he goes to get it, the sow will tear him in pieces."

Well (but not particularly well!), when Víťazko returned from the chase, bringing a buck for his mother, she groaned and complained: "Alas! my dear son, your toil has been in vain. It is no use your bringing me this good food; I cannot eat it, for I am deadly sick."

"Alas! mother, you must not die. Only tell me what would cure you, and I will bring it for you, even though it were from hell," cried the good Víťazko, for he loved his mother well.

" I can only be cured if I get the suckling of the earth sow."

Vítazko did not wait; he took his beech-tree and set off in quest of the earth sow. He wandered through the country, poor soul! for he did not know where to go, till at last he came to a tower, and there he found Holy Sunday.

"Where are you going?" asked Holy Sunday.

" I am going to the earth sow to get one of her sucklings. My mother is ill, but this will cure her."

" My dear boy, it will be a hard task for you to get that piglet. However, I will help you. Only you must follow my advice exactly."

Vítazko promised that he would follow it exactly. So first she gave him a long, sharp spit, and then she said:

"Go to the stable and take my horse. He will bring you to the place where the earth sow lies buried in the earth. When you have come there you must prick one of her pigs. The pig will squeak, and the sow, hearing it, will start up and run round the earth in a moment. But she won't see you or anybody else, and so she will tell the pigs that if they squeak again she will tear them to pieces. Then she will lie down to sleep, and then you must spit the pig and run quickly away. The pig will be afraid to squeak, the sow won't stir, and my horse will carry you away."

Víťazko promised to carry out her directions exactly. He took the spit, mounted the magic horse, and it brought him swiftly to the place—far, very far it was—where the earth sow lay buried in the earth. Víťazko pricked one of the pigs, and it squeaked terribly. The sow started wildly up and ran round the earth in one moment. But the magic horse did not move, so the sow did not see him or anybody else, and she said angrily to the pigs :

"If one of you squeaks, I will tear you all to pieces at once."

Having said this, she buried herself again.

At once Víťazko spitted the pig. It kept quiet and didn't squeak at all, and the magic horse began to fly, and it wasn't long till they were home again.

"Well, Víťazko, how did it go?" asked Holy Sunday.

"Well, it went just as you said, and here is the pig."

"Very well. Take it to your mother."

Víťazko gave her back the spit; he led the magic horse back to its stall, thanked Holy Sunday, and, hanging the pig from the beech-tree, made haste to go home to his mother.

The mother and the griffin were feasting; they did not expect Víťazko, and here he was. They ran away and discussed what they should do with him.

"When he has given you the pig, you must still pretend to be ill," said the griffin; "and when he asks you what will save you, tell him that only the Water of Life and the Water of Death can cure you. If he goes in quest of that, he is bound to perish."

Víťazko came running to the castle full of joy. He gave the pig to his mother, but she still went on groaning and complaining that she was going to die, and that the pig would not cure her.

"Alas! mother, don't die, but tell me what will cure you, so that I may bring it for you at once," said Víťazko anxiously.

"Ah! my dear son, I can only be cured

by the Water of Life and the Water of
Death, and where would you get that?"
sighed the mother.

Víťazko did not waste time thinking about
it. He grasped his beech, and off he went
to Holy Sunday.

"Where are you going, Víťazko?" asked
Holy Sunday.

"I am coming to you to ask where I
could find the Water of Life and the Water
of Death, for my mother is still ill, and only
those will cure her."

"It will be a hard task for you to get them,
but I will help you as well as I can. Here
are two jugs; mount my magic horse, and
he will bring you to two banks. Beneath
those two banks spring forth the Water of
Life and the Water of Death. The right
bank opens at noon, and from beneath it
gushes the Water of Life. The left bank
opens at midnight, and beneath it is the
Water of Death. As soon as the bank opens,
run up to it and fill your jug with water,
and so you must do in the other case too.
When you have the water, come back.
Follow my instructions carefully."

Saying this, she gave him two jugs. He

took them and mounted the magic horse, and
in a moment they were gone like the wind.
The two banks were in a far distant land,
and thither the magic horse brought Víťazko.
At noon he raised the right bank and the
Water of Life gushed forth, then, crash! the
bank fell down again, and it was a wonder
that it did not take Víťazko's heels off.
Quickly Víťazko mounted the magic horse
and made haste for the left bank. There
they waited till midnight. When the bank
lifted, beneath it was the Water of Death.
He hurried to it and filled the jug, and,
crash! down fell the bank again; and it was
a marvel it didn't take Víťazko's hand off.
Quickly he mounted the magic horse, the
horse flew off, and soon they were home
again.

"Well, Víťazko, how have you fared?"
asked Holy Sunday.

"Oh! everything went all right, Holy
Sunday; and here is the water," said Víťazko,
giving her the water.

Holy Sunday kept the water, and gave
him two jugs full of spring water and told
him to take them to his mother. Víťazko
thanked her and went home.

The mother and the griffin were carousing
as before, for they did not expect that he
would ever return—and there he was just
outside. They were terribly frightened, and
considered how they could get rid of him.

"You must pretend to be sick still, and
tell him you won't recover unless you get
the Pelican bird, and he will perish on the
quest," said the griffin.

Vítazko brought the water joyfully, but the
mother was still groaning and complaining;
even that was no good, she was sure she
was going to die.

"Ah! don't die, sweet mother. Tell me
what will cure you, and I shall be glad to
get it all for you," said the good lad.

"There is no help for me unless I can
see the Pelican bird. Where could you get
it for me?" groaned the mother.

Vítazko took his beech again, and it was
no trouble to him to go to Holy Sunday
once more.

"Where are you going?" asked Holy
Sunday.

"Well, I am coming to you to ask for
advice. Mother is still sick; the water did
not cure her either, and she says she must

see the Pelican bird. And where is the Pelican bird?"

"My dear child, it would be very hard for you to get the Pelican bird. But I will help you all I can. The Pelican bird is a gigantic bird. His neck is very long, and, whenever he shakes his wings, he raises such a wind that the trees begin to shake. Here is a gun; mount my magic horse, and he will bring you to the place where the Pelican bird lives. But be careful. Point the gun against the wind from whatever quarter it blows, and when the hammer falls, ram the gun with the ramrod and come quickly back. You must not look into the gun."

Vítazko took the gun and mounted the magic horse, and the horse spread his wings, and they were flying through the air a long way until they came to a vast desert, where dwelt the Pelican bird. There the magic horse stopped. Now Vítazko perceived that the wind was blowing strongly on his left cheek, so he pointed the gun in that direction, and, clap! the hammer fell. Vítazko rammed the gun quickly with the ramrod and flung it over his shoulder, and the horse started flying, and very soon they were home again.

" Well, how did things go ? "

" I don't know whether they went well or ill, but I did what you commanded," answered Víťazko, handing down the gun to Holy Sunday.

" All right. You did quite right. Here he is ! " she said. And then she took out the Pelican bird. Then she gave Víťazko another gun to shoot an eagle with. He went out into the forest, and returned before long with an eagle. She gave him this eagle for his mother, in place of the Pelican bird.

The griffin and the mother were making merry again, hoping that Víťazko would never come back, but he was already near. They were terrified, and began to consider what new task they were to set him.

" You must pretend to be sick still, and tell him nothing can do you any good but the golden apples from the garden of the Griffin. If he goes there the Griffin will tear him in pieces, for he is enraged because Víťazko has killed his brothers."

Joyfully Víťazko gave the bird to his mother, but she still kept on groaning; nothing was any good, only the golden apples from the garden of the Griffin could save her.

"You shall have them," said Vítazko, and without resting, he started again and came to Holy Sunday.

"Where are you going, Vítazko?"

"Well," he replied, "not even that did her any good. Mother is still sick, for only the golden apples from the garden of the Griffin will cure her."

"Well, you'll have to fight, my boy," said Holy Sunday; "but, even though you were stronger than you are, it would be a bad look-out for you. Still, I will help you all I can. Here is a ring for you; put it on your finger, and, when you are in need, think of me, turn the ring round on your finger, and you will have the strength of a hundred men. Now mount the magic horse; he will take you there."

Vítazko thanked her heartily, mounted the magic horse, and was carried by him a far journey, till they came to a garden hedged about by a high rampart. Had it not been for the magic horse Vítazko could never have got into the garden, but the horse flew like a bird over the rampart. Vítazko leapt down from the horse, and instantly began to look for a tree with golden apples. A beautiful girl met him and asked him what he was looking for. Viťazko said that he was looking for golden apples to cure his sick mother, and begged her to tell him where to look for them.

"The apple-tree is under my charge, and I must not give the apples to anybody, or the Griffin would tear me to pieces. I am a king's daughter, and the Griffin carried me off and brought me to this garden and put me in charge of the apples. Go back, good youth, go back, for the Griffin is very strong, and, if he sees you, he will kill you like a fly," said the girl.

But Viťazko was not to be turned back, and he hastened on into the garden. So the princess pulled off a priceless ring and handed it to Viťazko, saying: "Take this ring, and when you think of me and turn this ring round on your finger, you will have the strength of a hundred men, otherwise you could not gain the victory over the Griffin."

Viťazko took the ring and put it on his finger. He thanked her and went off to the

centre of the garden.   In the middle of the
garden stood an apple-tree full of golden
apples, and underneath it a horrible Griffin
was lying.

"What do you want here, murderer of my
brothers?" shouted the Griffin.

"I have come to get some apples from
this tree," answered Vítazko undauntedly.

"You shall not have any of the apples
unless you wrestle with me," exclaimed the
Griffin angrily.

"I will if you like.   Come on!" said
Vítazko, and he turned the ring on his right
hand and thought of Holy Sunday.   He set
his legs wide apart and they began to wrestle.
In the first round the Griffin moved Vítazko
a little, but Vítazko drove him into the ground
above his ankles.   Just at this moment they
heard a swirl of wings above them, and a
black raven shouted to them :

"Which am I to help, the Griffin or
Vítazko?"

"Help me," said the Griffin.

"And what will you give me?"

"I will give you gold and silver as much
as you like."

"Help me," cried Vítazko, "and I will

give you all those horses grazing on yonder
meadow."

"I will help you, then," said the raven.
"But how am I to help you?"

"Cool me when I grow hot," said Víťazko.
He felt hot indeed, for the Griffin was breath-
ing out fire against him. So they went on
wrestling. The Griffin seized Víťazko and
drove him into the ground up to his ankles.
Víťazko turned the ring, and again he thought
of Holy Sunday. He put his arms round
the Griffin's waist and drove him down into
the ground above his knees. The black
raven dipped his wings in a spring, and then
he alighted on Víťazko's head and sprinkled
cool drops over Víťazko's hot cheeks, and thus
he cooled him. Then Víťazko turned the
other ring and thought of the beautiful maiden,
and they began wrestling again. So the
Griffin drove Víťazko into the ground up to
his ankles, but Víťazko took hold of him and
drove him into the ground up to his shoulders,
and quickly he seized his sword, the gift of
Holy Sunday, and cut the Griffin's head off.

The princess came to him at once and
plucked the golden apples for him. She
thanked him too for delivering her, and said

that she liked him well and she would marry him.

"I like you well too," confessed Víťazko, " and, if I could, I would go with you at once. But if you really love me, and if you will consent to wait a year for me, I will come to you then."

The princess pledged herself by shaking hands with him, and she said she would wait a year for him. And so they said good-bye to each other. Víťazko mounted his horse, cleared the rampart at a leap, killed the horses on the meadow for the black raven, and hastened home.

"Well, how have you fared?" asked Holy Sunday.

"Very well, but if it hadn't been for a ring which was given me by a princess I should have fared very badly," answered Víťazko, and he told her everything. She told him to go home with the golden apples and to take the magic horse with him too. Víťazko obeyed.

The griffin and the mother were carousing again. They were greatly startled when Víťazko came riding home; they had never expected that he would return alive even from the garden of the Griffin. The mother asked what she should do; but the griffin had no more shifts; he made off to the tenth room at once and hid himself there. When Víťazko had given the apples to his mother, she pretended that the mere sight of them had cured her, and, rising from the bed, she put the finest of food before Víťazko and then began to caress him as she used to do sometimes when he was a tiny baby. Víťazko was delighted to see his mother in good health again. The mother took a strong cotton cord and said jestingly: "Lie down, dear son; I will wind this cord round you as I used to wind it round your father, to see if you are as strong as he was, and if you can break it."

Víťazko smiled and laid himself down, and allowed his mother to wind the cord round him. When she had finished, he stretched his limbs and snapt the cord in pieces.

"You are strong," she said. "But wait! I will wind this thin silk cord round you to see if you can break it also."

So she did. Víťazko tried to stretch his limbs, but the more he stretched, the deeper

the cord cut into him. So he was helpless,
and had to lie like a baby in its swaddling-
clothes. Now the griffin hastened to cut his
head off; he hewed the body in pieces and
hung the heart from the ceiling. The mother
packed the body in a cloth, and put the bundle
on the back of the magic horse, which was
waiting in the courtyard, saying :

"You carried him alive, so you can carry
him dead too, wherever you like."

The horse did not wait, but flew off, and
soon they reached home.

Holy Sunday had been expecting him, for
she knew what would probably happen to
him. Without delay she rubbed the body
with the Water of Death, then she put it
together and poured the Water of Life over
it. Vítazko yawned, and rose to his feet alive
and well. "Well, I have had a long sleep,"
he said to himself.

"You would have been sleeping till doomsday if I hadn't awakened you. Well, how
do you feel now?"

"Oh! I am all right! Only, it's funny: it's
as though I had not got any heart."

"That is true; you haven't got a heart,"
answered Holy Sunday.

" Where can it be, then ? "

" Where else should it be, but in the castle,
hanging from the crossbeam ? " said Holy
Sunday, and she told him all that had
happened to him.

But Víťazko could not be angry, neither
could he weep, for he had no heart. So he
had to go and get it. Holy Sunday gave
him a fiddle and sent him to the castle.
He was to play on the fiddle, and, as a
reward, was to ask for the heart, and, when
he got it, he must return at once to Holy
Sunday—those were her orders.

Víťazko went to the castle, and when he
saw that his mother was looking out of the
window, he began playing beautifully. The
mother was delighted with the music below,
so she called the old fiddler (for Holy Sunday
had put that shape upon him) into the castle
and asked him to play. He played, and the
mother danced with the griffin ; they danced
hard, and did not stop until they were tired.
Then the mother gave the fiddler meat and
drink, and she offered him gold, but he would
not take it.

" What could I do with all that money ?
I am too old for it," he answered.

"Well, what am I to give you, then? It is for you to ask," said the mother.

"What are you to give me?" said he, looking round the room. "Oh! give me that heart, hanging there from the crossbeam!"

"If you like that, we can give it to you," said the griffin, and the mother took it down and gave it to Víťazko. He thanked them for it, and hastened from the castle to Holy Sunday.

"It is lucky that we have got it again," said Holy Sunday; and she took the heart in her hands, washed it first in the Water of Death and afterwards in the Water of Life, and then she put it in the bill of the Pelican bird. The bird stretched out his long neck and replaced the heart in Víťazko's breast. At once Víťazko felt it joyfully leaping. And for this service Holy Sunday gave the Pelican bird his freedom again.

And now she said to Víťazko: "You must go once more to the castle and deal out justice. Take the form of a pigeon and, when you think of me, you will regain your own shape."

No sooner had she said this than Víťazko was changed into a pigeon, and away he flew to the castle. The mother and the griffin were caressing each other when suddenly a pigeon alighted on the window-sill. As soon as the mother saw the pigeon she sent the griffin to shoot him, but before the griffin could get hold of his crossbow the pigeon flew down into the hall, took human form, seized the sword and cut the griffin's head off at a stroke.

"And what am I to do with thee, thou good-for-nothing mother?" he said, turning to his mother, who in terror fell at his feet begging for mercy. "Do not be afraid—I will not do you any harm. Let God judge between us." He took her hand and led her to the castle yard, unsheathed his sword, and said: "Behold, mother! I will throw this sword into the air. If I am guilty, it will strike me; if you are guilty, it is you it will strike. Let God decide."

The sword whirled through the air, it darted past Vítazko's head, and smote straight into his mother's heart.

Vítazko lamented over her and buried her. Then he returned to Holy Sunday and thanked her well for all her kindness. He girded on the sword, took his beech-tree in his hand, and went to his beautiful princess. He found her with her royal father, who had tried to make her marry various kings and princes, but she would marry none of them. She would wait a year, she said. The year was not yet over when one day Vítazko arrived in the royal palace to ask for the maiden's hand.

"This is my betrothed," exclaimed the princess joyfully, as soon as she saw him, and she went straight up to him.

A splendid feast was made ready, the father gave his kingdom into their hands, and that is the end of this story.

BOOTS, CLOAK, AND RING

ONCE there was a blacksmith, and he had only one son, John by name. They sent him to school, but fortune changed and his parents fell into poverty, so they were forced to take their son home again. John had already passed through the higher standard, but he could not support his parents. So one day he said:

"Father and mother! What can I do at home? There is no business here, so I can't be a clerk, and I am too old now to learn a trade. So I will go out into the world and find myself a job, and, whenever I can, I will send you some money. And when I get a good job, you must sell your cottage and come and live with me."

His father and mother wept, because he wanted to leave them, but they knew that he was right, for there was no chance for him if he stayed at home. So they let him go.

They gave him their blessing before he went out into the world. John wept till his heart nearly broke at parting with his aged parents.

He walked on till noon. At noon he sat down beneath a lime-tree beside a well, and had his meal and a drink. Then, strengthened and refreshed, he walked on till nightfall. The country was quite unknown to him, so he had to spend the night in the forest. The next day he went on again till he came into a wild mountain country. There he stopped and thought over what he should do next. He stood awhile, and then he went on again. He reached a pleasant valley, and there he found three brothers. They were quarrelling and on the point of coming to blows. John asked them what the matter was. The eldest answered :

"Our father has died, and he bequeathed to us these boots, this cloak, and this hat. And each of us would like to own the boots."

"Why?" asked John.

"Because they have the property that whoever puts them on can cover ten miles in the moment he wishes it. The cloak has the property that its owner can fly as far and as high as he likes. And the property of the hat is that it makes its wearer invisible."

John said: "You are brothers, and you ought not to quarrel. You must love one another. So that you won't quarrel any more, I will decide the matter for you. Give me those things."

They gave him the boots, the cloak, and the hat. He put the hat on, and they couldn't see him any more; he wrapped himself in the cloak, took the boots, and flew away.

He flew some distance before he alighted upon a log and put the boots on. As he sat on the log, it turned over, and he saw a big hole under it. He went down the hole and came to some stairs, and went down them to the bottom without any difficulty. There he found a big room without any human being in it. The table was laid for one person. He thought: " I am hungry. Shall I eat this meal?" Finally he decided to risk it; he took off his hat and began to eat.

When he had finished, an old crone entered the room, and asked: " Did you like your meal?"

" Oh, it was very nice indeed," answered John ; "and, by the way, could you give me lodging for the night?"

" I will, if you can stand it ; for at midnight twenty-four ghosts will come, and they will try to make you play cards with them and dance with them. But you must sit still and not so much as look at them."

So the first night came. John was sitting eating his meal. When he had finished, he remained at table. After eleven o'clock two dozen ghosts entered the room and asked him to play cards with them. He refused, so they began preparations for playing skittles, and again asked him to join them, but he would not. Then a delightful music began to play, and they asked him to dance with them. No, he wouldn't ; he did not so much as look at them. They kept on dragging him about, tearing and biting him, till he began to think it was all over with him. But just then it struck twelve, and the ghosts vanished.

In the morning the old crone came back and waked him, for he was still asleep on the ground. She asked him : " How did you sleep ? "

" Very well," said John.

" Did you, now ? " answered the old woman. " Well, next night will be still worse, if you can stand it. Two score of ghosts will come, and they'll urge you to play cards and skittles with them and to dance with them. But you must sit quiet; don't so much as look at them."

He stayed there that day, and had a good time. Then the second night came. After eleven o'clock twoscore ghosts rushed in. They urged him to play cards and skittles with them and to dance with them. But John wouldn't. He sat still, without so much as looking at them. So they began to torture him again, and dragged him about even worse than before. But when it struck twelve they left him on the ground and disappeared.

In the morning the old crone came. She washed him with some lotion till he recovered. She asked him : " How did you sleep ? "

" Splendidly," said he.

" Did you, now ? " said she. " It was a bad lodging for you, but the third night will be even worse, if you can stand it. Three score of ghosts will come, and will urge you to play cards and skittles and to dance with them. But you must sit still and not so much as look at them."

All that day he had a good time again. The third night came, and after eleven o'clock three score of ghosts rushed in. They gathered round him, and urged, prayed, and besought him to play and dance with him. When he refused, they seized him and began knocking him against the ground, tearing and biting him, so that he lost his senses and did not see them go away.

In the morning the old crone came and anointed him with a precious salve till he recovered. The old woman said : " You wouldn't have had such a bad time if you had not stolen the boots, the cloak, and the hat. The ghosts would simply have pressed you ; they would have had no power over you. As you followed my advice and did not play with them, you have delivered an enchanted town and a beautiful princess. She will come to you at once. Now you are rich, return the stolen goods."

Then there came a girl in a white robe. It was the beautiful princess, and she thanked him for delivering her and the whole town.

He went to the window, and outside he saw streets full of people and soldiers and a great bustle going on. The princess said :

" My father is a king, and you will marry me and succeed him. But my father dwells far from here, and we will go to him. Do you take this ring here."

So they went off. When the wedding was to take place, John wanted his parents to be present, so he asked the princess : " May I go to see my parents ? I would like them to be at our wedding."

The princess answered : " They live a great way from us, but you will be able to get to them. The ring I gave you has the property that, when you turn it on your finger and wish to go a hundred miles, you will cover that distance in a moment. On your way you will come to a king who has a beautiful daughter. But you must not think of her nor of me, for then you will lose the ring, and you will not be able to go any farther."

John started. He turned the ring, and in a moment he was a hundred miles off, and found himself with a king who had several sons. They entertained him splendidly. Then

he came to another king who had an only
daughter, and she was very vulgar. The
king insisted that John should marry her.
John thought: "What are you thinking of,
my man? My bright one is so beautiful
that there is not her equal in the wide world,
while your daughter is only a vulgar creature." At the moment he thought of his
bride the ring slipped from his finger and
disappeared.

John left them then. He was very sad,
and considered what he should do. "My
bride is far away now," he thought. "I
cannot find my way either to her or to my
parents."

As he was walking along in this sad mood,
he thought of his cloak, and it came into
his mind that, if he could reach the Sun's
abode the same day, he could ask where his
bride's castle was. As soon as he thought
of this he was at the Sun's house. The
Sun was not in; only his housekeeper was at
home. He asked her for a lodging, and said
that he would like to ask the Sun whether
he knew the castle where his bride dwelt.
She gave him the lodging. When the Sun
returned home in the evening, John asked

him whether he had any knowledge of the castle in which his wife dwelt. The Sun answered: "I don't know. I never shone there. But go and ask the Moon."

The next day, as soon as he woke, he flew off on his cloak to the Moon's castle. When he got there, the Moon was not in, and John asked the housekeeper for a night's lodging. He said he would like to ask the Moon's advice.

The housekeeper said: "You must wait till the Moon comes home, but you will be very cold, for my mistress is an extremely cold person."

"I will crouch in a corner and wait till the mistress comes; in any case, my cloak is warm enough."

When the morning drew near, the Moon returned home, and John asked her whether she knew where his bride's castle was.

The Moon said: "I never shone there. But go to the Wind. He is a fellow who penetrates everywhere, and so he is likely to know where that castle is."

So John went to the Wind's house. The Wind was not in, but Melusine, his wife, was alone at home. John asked her to let him stay there for the night. She tried to dissuade him.

" It is impossible, good sir. My lord is used to blow terribly. It will be exceedingly cold."

He answered: " I will cover myself up and crouch somewhere. I can endure cold, and, anyhow, my cloak is warm enough." So he stayed there for the night.

After midnight the Wind came home and asked : " Who is here with you, wife? I smell a man."

" Who should be here ? " she said. " Your nose is still full of the human smell."

But the Wind persisted : " There is somebody here ! Tell me ! "

So she confessed. " Don't be angry, dear husband ! There is a man staying here for the night, and he wants to ask you whether you will be kind enough to take him to his bride's castle."

The Wind answered : " It is very far from here, and I must ask the Lord how strongly I am to blow, if we are to get there. I was there yesterday ; they are going to celebrate a wedding there, and they have been drying some shirts ready for it, and I have been helping them."

The Wind went to ask the Lord; and when he came back, he said to John: "I can blow strongly enough, but I don't know whether you will be able to keep step with me."

John answered: "I have got good boots, and I am sure I can."

So he wrapped himself in his cloak, covered his head with his hat, and put his boots on, and he went ahead so quickly that the Wind could hardly keep step with him. As they drew near to the castle, the Wind said: "Here it is," and disappeared in a whirl.

The other bridegroom had already arrived, and was at the wedding feast. John passed through the castle, and came to the table at which they were dining. Nobody could see him. He remained standing near the bride, and whenever she lifted the food to her mouth, he ate it before it could reach her mouth, so that the spoon reached her mouth empty.

After the banquet she said: "My plates were well filled, and yet it is as though I had been eating nothing at all. Who is it that has eaten my food? My glass was full too. I have not drunk, and yet it is empty. Who has drunk my wine?"

Then she went to the kitchen, and John followed close at her heels. When she was alone he revealed himself. He took his hat off, and she knew him. She was greatly rejoiced at this, and ran to the room and said :

"Gentlemen, I would like to ask you a question. I had a golden key and I lost it. So I had a silver key made for me, and, now that it is made, I have found the golden key. Would you be so kind as to advise me which of them I ought to keep?"

The bridegroom stepped forward and said : "Keep the golden key."

Off she went. She dressed John in beautiful garments, and then presented him to the guests, saying : "This is my golden key. He delivered me from torment, and I was to marry him. He went to see his parents, but he could not reach them. Now he has come back to me just as I was going to marry another man, the silver key of my story, though I had given up all hope of his return. Yet he has come back, and I shall keep him, the golden key, for the silver key has himself decided so."

The wedding was celebrated the next day, and John took charge of the old king's kingdom. Then they both went to visit his old parents, and brought them back with them to the palace. On their way back they called on the three brothers, and John gave them back the boots, the cloak, and the hat. And if they haven't died since, they are still alive enjoying their kingdom.

[Intentionally Left Blank]

52

[Intentionally Left Blank]

53

SILLY JURA

ONCE there were two brothers. They were lazy fellows, and thieves into the bargain. They were expected to give a feast. They said to one another : " We haven't got anything. Wherever shall we find food for the feast ? "

So the first said : " I'll go to our neighbour's. He has some fine apples, and I'll pluck some of them."

The second said : " I'll go to the shepherd's. He has some fine rams. I'll steal a ram from him."

These two brothers hated the third, and so they abused him : " Silly Jura ! You won't get anything yourself, but you'll be ready enough to eat what we get."

So Jura said : " I'll go to the burgomaster's and get some nuts."

In the evening they went their ways. When he had finished plucking the nuts,

Jura went into the charnel-house at the back of the church and began to crack the nuts there. The watchmen heard the cracking in the charnel-house, and they thought the place was haunted. As there was no priest in the village (he lived in the next village), they went to the burgomaster and asked him to go with them to the charnel-house, saying that the place was haunted.

The burgomaster said : " I am so ill that I can't stand on my feet ; no doctor can help me."

But the watchmen insisted, and so the burgomaster told his servant to take him on his back and carry him to the place. The servant carried him along, and the watchmen called at the churchwarden's to ask for some holy water.

When they came near to the charnel-house, Jura thought it was his brother bringing the ram, so he called out : "Are you bringing him ? "

The servant was frightened, and let the burgomaster fall and ran away. The burgomaster was terrified too. He jumped up and ran after the servant. He cleared a wooden fence with one leap in his flight, and it wasn't long till he reached home. His family wondered to see him cured so quickly without the help of a doctor.

Next day the burgomaster proclaimed that he would give a pound to the man who had stolen his nuts the day before, if he would only come to see him. So Jura went to him, and the burgomaster said : "I ought to punish you for stealing, but since you have cured my illness which nobody was able to cure, I'll give you the pound I promised, but you mustn't steal any more." So Jura promised not to steal any more, and went home.

The brothers grew very fond of him now that he had money. They borrowed the money from him and bought themselves new clothes, and said : "We'll go to see the world and to get wives for ourselves. As for you, Silly Jura, you must stay at home ; you'd never get a good wife for yourself."

So off they went. But Jura went too. He went to the forest and he was utterly dazzled. He had often heard that there was an enchanted castle in that forest. When he came to the place where the ruins of the castle were, night overtook him, and so he could see nothing except what looked like a light in a cellar. So he went into the cellar to make his night's lodging there. There was nobody in the cellar but a cat. The cat greeted him : "Welcome, dear Jura ! How did you come here ? "

Jura was frightened when he heard the cat speak, and was going to run away. But the cat told him not to go ; there was no need to be frightened. He must come back, and no harm would be done to him. If he wanted to eat, he could go into the storeroom and take what he wanted. She would take him for her servant.

So he stayed there a year and had a good time. He never saw a cook, but he always found meals ready prepared in the storeroom. He had nothing to do but get firewood, and at the end of the year he was told to make a great pile of it. Then the cat said : " You must light the pile to-day, and throw me into the fire. You must not help me out, however I entreat you, but you must let me be consumed."

Jura answered : " I can't do that. I have had a good time with you. Why should I repay you in such an evil way ? "

The cat said : " If you don't do as I have said, you will be very unhappy. If you do it, you will be happy."

So Jura kindled the pile, and, when it was well alight, he picked up the cat and threw her into the fire. She wanted to escape from the fire, but he wouldn't let her go. At last he was so weary that he was forced to lie down, and soon he fell asleep. When he awoke, he opened his eyes, and behold! there was no ruin ; he heard delightful music and saw a beautiful palace with crowds of servants. He was wondering at all this, when a splendidly dressed lady came up to him and asked him if he did not know her.

Jura said : " How should I know your ladyship? I never saw you before in my life."

The lady said : " I am that cat. Witches had put me under enchantment in the shape of a cat. Now we will go after your brothers who hated you so much and see how they are getting on."

She ordered her people to dress him in fine clothes, a fine carriage was prepared, and they drove off. As they were approaching the village, the lady said to her bridegroom :

"Put your old clothes on." Then she called an old, ragged beggarwoman and sent him with her. She herself remained outside of the village.

When the brothers saw Jura coming with the ragged beggarwoman, they shouted : "He is bringing home an old ragged bride, and he's in rags too." The other brothers were married too, and they were pretty badly off, so they turned him out and wouldn't have him at home.

So Jura went out of the village ; he changed his clothes and drove back with the lady to his brothers' cottage. When the carriage stopped before the cottage, the brothers said : "What a fine carriage ! Who is that noble lord and the beautiful lady who have come to our cottage?" They did not recognize their brother.

So she said : "Look here. You were always hard on your brother, always sneering at him, and now you are badly off enough, while he is getting on splendidly. If you mend your ways, you will get on too."

Afterwards she gave them some money and went away with Jura.

SLEEPY JOHN

ONCE there was a lad named John, and he used to go to sleep always and everywhere. One day he came to an inn where some farmers were feeding their horses. So he crept into the cart, lay down on the straw, and went to sleep. When the farmers had driven some distance, they noticed John asleep in the cart. They thought : " What are we to do with him ? We have a beer cask here. We'll put him in it and leave him in the forest." So they shut him in the cask, and off they drove.

John went on sleeping in the cask for a long time. Suddenly he woke up and found himself in the cask, but he did not know how he had got into it, neither did he know where he was. There was something running to and fro near the cask, so he looked through the bunghole and saw a great number of wolves gathered under the rocks. They had flocked round, attracted by the human smell. One of the wolves pushed his tail through the hole, and Sleepy John began to think that the hour of his death was approaching. But he wound the wolf's tail round his hand. The wolf was terrified, and, dragging the cask after him, he ran after the rest of the wolves, who set off in all directions. Their terror grew greater and greater as the cask bumped after them. At last the cask struck against a rock and was smashed. John let go the wolf, who took himself off as fast as he could.

Now John found himself in a wild mountain region. He began walking about among the mountains and he met a hermit. The hermit said to him : " You may stay here with me. I shall die in three days. Bury me then, and I will pay you well for it."

So John stayed with him, and, when the third day came, the hermit, who was about to die, gave him a stick, saying : " In whatever direction you point this stick, you will find yourself there." Then he gave him a knapsack, saying : "Anything you want you will find in this knapsack." Then he gave him a cap, saying : " As soon as you put this cap on, nobody will be able to see you."

Then the hermit died, and John buried him.

John gathered his things together, pointed the stick, and said : " Let me be instantly in the town where the king lives." He found himself there on the instant, and he was told that the queen would every night wear out a dozen pairs of shoes, yet nobody was able to follow her track. The lords were all flocking to offer to follow the queen's traces, and John went too. He went into the palace and had himself announced to the king. When he came before the king, he said that he would like to trace the queen. The king asked him : " Who are you ? "

He answered "Sleepy John."

The king said : " And how are you going to trace her, when you are sleeping all the time? If you fail to trace her you will lose your head."

John answered that he would try to trace her all the same.

When the evening was come the queen went to bed in one room and John went to bed in the next room, through which the queen had to pass. He did not go to sleep, but when the queen was going by he pretended to be in a deep slumber. So the queen lit a candle and scorched the soles of his feet to make sure that he was asleep. But John didn't stir, and so she was certain that he was asleep. Then she took her twelve pairs of new shoes and off she went.

John got up, put his cap on, and pointed with his stick and said : " Let me be where the queen is."

Now, when the queen came to a certain rock, the earth opened before her and two dragons came to meet her. They took her on their backs and carried her as far as the lead forest. Then John said : " Let me be where the queen is," and instantly he was in the lead forest. So he broke off a twig for a proof and put it in his knapsack. But when he broke off the twig it gave out a shrill sound as if a bell were ringing. The queen was frightened, but she rode on again. John pointed with his stick and said : " Let me be where the queen is," and instantly he was in the tin forest. He broke off a twig again and put it in his knapsack, and it rang again. The queen turned pale, but she rode on again. John pointed with his stick again and said : "Let me be where the queen is," and instantly he was in the silver forest. He broke off a twig again and put it into his knapsack. As he broke it, it gave out a ringing sound and the queen fainted. The dragons hastened on again till they came to a green meadow.

A crowd of devils came to meet them here, and they revived the queen. Then they had a feast. Sleepy John was there too. The cook was not at home that day, so John sat down in his place, and, as he had his cap on, nobody could see him. They put aside a part of the food for the cook, but John ate it all. They were all surprised to see all the food they put aside disappearing. They couldn't make out what was happening, but they didn't care very much. And when the banquet was at an end the devils began to dance with the queen, and they kept on dancing until the queen had worn out all her shoes. When her shoes were worn out, those two dragons took her on their backs again and brought her to the place where the earth had opened before her. John said : "Let me be where the queen is." By this time she was walking on the earth again, and he followed her. When they came near the palace he went ahead of the queen and went to bed; and, as the queen was going in, she saw him sleeping, and so she went to her own room and lay down and slept.

In the morning the lords gathered together and the king asked whether any of them had tracked the queen. But none of them could say "Yes."

So he summoned Sleepy John before him. John said:

"Gracious Lord King, I did indeed track her, and I know that she used up those twelve pairs of shoes upon the green meadows in Hell."

The queen stood forth at once, and John took from his knapsack the leaden twig and said: "The queen was carried by two dragons towards Hell, and she came to the leaden forest; there I broke off this twig and the queen was frightened."

The king said: "That's no good. You might have made the twig yourself."

So John produced the tin twig from his knapsack and said: "After that the queen drove through the tin forest, and there I broke off this twig. That time the queen grew pale."

The king said: "You might have made even this twig."

So John produced the silver twig and said: "Afterwards the queen drove through the silver forest, and when I broke off this twig she fainted, and so she was until the devils brought her to life again."

The queen, seeing that all was known, cried out: "Let the earth swallow me!" and she was swallowed by the earth.

Sleepy John got the half of the kingdom, and, when the king died, the other half too.

[Intentionally Left Blank]
68

[Intentionally Left Blank]
69

THREE DOVES

A CERTAIN merchant died. His son was nineteen years old at the time. He said to his mother: "Mother dear, I'm going to try my luck in the world."

His mother answered: "Go, dear son, but don't stay long there, for I am old, and should like some help in my old age." She fitted him out for the journey, and said good-bye to him.

Out into the world went the son, and he travelled on till he came into a forest. He had been going through it for three days, and no end appeared. On the third day he kept on and came at last to a cottage. He went into the cottage and he saw a horrible being seated on a stool. The fellow asked him where he was going.

"I don't know where I am going. I'm seeking my fortune in some service."

"Well, if you like, you can enter my service."

The lad was very hungry, so he took service with the other.

His master said to him : "You must serve me for a year at least."

So he served him for a year. He was treated very well, and he was a faithful servant to his master. The master was a sorcerer, but he didn't do any harm to the lad. He had a big pond, and three doves used to come there to bathe. Each of them had three golden feathers. These three doves were three enchanted princesses.

When the year's service was ended, the sorcerer said : "What wages shall I give you ? "

The lad said he left it to him.

"You're a good lad," said the sorcerer. "Come with me to my cellar and take as much money as you like, gold or silver, just as you wish."

So the lad took as much as he could carry, and the sorcerer gave him one of the three doves too, saying :

"When you get home, if you haven't got a house of your own, have one built, and then pluck those three feathers out of the dove, and hide them away so carefully that no human

eye can see them. The dove will turn into
a lovely princess and you may marry her."

So he took the dove and returned home.
He had a house built and made a secret place
in one of the walls for the three feathers.
When he plucked out the feathers the dove
became a beautiful princess, but she did not
know where the feathers were. But his mother
knew quite well, for he had told her all and
showed her where the feathers were hidden.

When they had been living together for
three years he went a-hunting one day with
another lord, and his mother stayed at home
with her daughter-in-law. The mother said
to her : " Dear daughter-in-law, I can't tell
you how beautiful I think you. If one were
to search the whole world through, one couldn't
find so beautiful a woman."

The daughter-in-law answered : " Dear lady,
the beauty I have now is nothing to what I
should have had I but one of my golden
feathers."

The mother went straight off, fetched one
of the feathers, and gave it to her.

She thrust it into her skin, and she was
immediately far more beautiful than before.
The mother kept looking at her, and said :

" If you had the others as well, you would be even more beautiful." Then she fetched the other two feathers and gave them to her.

She thrust them into her skin, and behold! she was a dove again. She flew off through the window, thanking her mother-in-law: " Thank you, dearest mother, for giving me these three feathers. I will wait a little for my husband, to say good-bye to him."

So she perched on the roof to wait till her husband should return from the forest.

Now, the husband's nose fell to bleeding violently. He grew frightened, and began to wonder what great misfortune had befallen him at home. He mounted his horse and hastened home. As he was approaching the door the dove called out: " Good-bye, dear husband. I thank you for your true love, but you will never see me more."

Then the dove flew away, and the husband began to weep and to wail. Of course, he was very angry with his mother, and he decided to go away again and follow wherever his eyes might lead him. So he started off, and he went back to the sorcerer in whose service he had been before. As soon as he entered the sorcerer said :

"Aha! you have not followed my advice. I won't help you this time; the three doves are gone from here. But go to my brother, for all the birds and animals are under his power, and perhaps some of them might know where the doves are. I will give you a ball, and when you roll it three times, you will get there this evening. You must ask him whether he knows anything about the doves, and you must tell him, too, that I sent you to him."

The lad thanked him heartily and went on his way. He rolled the ball thrice and reached the other brother's by evening. He told him that his brother had asked to be remembered kindly to him, and then he asked whether he knew where the doves that used to bathe in his brother's pond were.

The brother answered: "My good lad, I know nothing at all about them. You must wait till morning. All the birds and animals are under my power, and if they know anything about it, it will be all right."

In the morning they went to the forest. The brother blew a whistle, and instantly swarms of birds gathered round, asking what was their master's will.

He said: "Tell me, does any one of you know about those three golden doves which used to bathe in my brother's pond?"

None of them knew, so he blew his whistle again and all manner of animals gathered round him: bears, lions, squirrels, wolves, every kind of wild animal, and they asked what was their master's will.

He said: "I would know whether any one of you knows anything about three golden doves which used to bathe in my brother's pond."

None of them knew. So he said:

"My dear lad, I cannot help you any more in this matter, but I have another brother, and, if he cannot tell you anything about them, then you will never hear of them any more. He dwells twice seventy miles from here, and all the devils of Hell are subjected to him. I will give you another ball like the one you had yesterday, and, when you have rolled it thrice, you will get there before evening."

He rolled the ball thrice and got there the same evening. The sorcerer was sitting in his garden on the grass. His hair was all dishevelled like a mop, his paunch was bare like a pail, his nose reached to his middle, and was as bare as a stick—in fact, his appearance was terrible.

The lad was terrified, but the sorcerer said: " Don't be frightened, my boy; though I look so hideous, yet I have a good heart. What do you want?"

"I have come from your brother to ask whether you can tell me about the three doves which used to bathe in your brother's pond."

" My dear lad, I know nothing about them, but as soon as you get up in the morning I will call my apprentices, to find if any one of them knows anything about the doves."

In the morning they got up and went into the forest. The sorcerer blew a whistle, and at once hosts of devils appeared, such a multitude that they darkened the whole forest.

The lad was frightened, but the sorcerer said: "Don't be afraid; not a hair of your head shall be harmed."

The devils asked what was their master's will.

He said: "Does any one of you know anything about the three doves which used to bathe in my brother's pond?"

None of them knew anything. The sorcerer looked about him and asked: "Where is the lame one?"

The lame one had been left behind, but he was hurrying up for fear he should be too late. He came and asked what was his master's will. The sorcerer answered: "I want to find out whether you know anything about those three doves that used to bathe in my brother's pond."

"Of course I know about them, for I have been driving them before me. They are bathing in the Red Sea now."

The sorcerer said: "You must take up this man and carry him as far as their gold-roofed palace," and he took the lad aside and whispered in his ear:

"When the devil asks you how quick he is to take you, if he says: 'As quickly as the wind blows?' say 'No'; and if he says, 'As quickly as the step goes?' say 'No' again. But if he says, 'As quickly as the air goes?' say 'Even so.' If your cap falls, do not look after it, and don't tell the devil about it, or he will let you fall and won't carry you to the palace. When you are seven miles from the palace you will see it, and the devil will ask you if you see it; but shut your eyes tight and say that you can't see it. When you are three miles from it, you will see it quite plainly, and he will ask you again whether you see it. But you must shut your eyes tight and say that you can't see it. Then you will be above the palace roof, and he will ask you again whether you see it. You must say again that you can't see it, or he will let you drop on the roof and you won't be able to get down."

The devil took the man and flew with him as the air goes. When they were seven miles from the palace, the devil asked: "Do you see the palace now? It is quite plain to see now."

The lad shut his eyes tight and said that he couldn't see it. So they flew on, and when they were three miles from the castle the devil asked him did he see it now. He shut his eyes tight and said that he couldn't see it. When they were right over the roof, the devil asked: "Surely you must see it now; we are just over the roof."

But he shut his eyes tight and said: "I don't see it."

The devil said angrily: "You must be

blind if you can't see it; we are just above the roof." And he seized him in anger, and set him on the golden table in that royal castle.

The three princesses were sitting at the table, knitting with golden thread. His own wife was the middle one, and she knew him at once. She sprang up right gladly and welcomed him with joy. She nearly fainted, she was so pleased that he had been able to come so many miles in such a short time.

"Welcome, dear husband, welcome! Welcome, our deliverer! You will save us from the enchantment under which we are in this castle."

The time passed very slowly there. So one day his wife brought him the keys and showed him through all the rooms and closets, letting him see everything except one room, which she would not open for him.

The three princesses had to take the shape of doves for two hours in the morning and three hours before the evening, and they had to go to the Red Sea to bathe there. One day when they had gone out to bathe he thought: "Why don't you want to open that room for me?" So he went and searched among the other keys for the key, and opened the room for himself.

In the room he saw a three-headed dragon, and each of its heads was stuck upon a hook so that it hung down from it. Under the dragon were placed three glasses of water. The lad was terrified and started to run away. But the dragon kept on calling out: "Don't be frightened, don't run away, but come back again and give me that glass of water. Your life shall be spared this once."

So he gave him the glass of water; the dragon drained it up, and instantly one of the heads fell from the hook. He begged again: "Now give me that other glass of water, and your life shall be spared a second time."

He gave it him; the dragon drank it up, and immediately the second head fell from the hook. Then the dragon said: "Now do as you like. But you must give me the third glass of water, whether you like it or not!"

In terror he gave him the third glass; the third head drank it up and fell from its hook. Now the dragon was quite free, and instantly he made for the Red Sea, and began to chase after the three doves until he caught one of them. It was the lad's wife.

The other two princesses came back again and began to weep and to wail.

"Thou luckless fellow! we were happy in the hope that thou wouldst deliver us, and now we are worse off than ever—now our torments will last till doomsday!"

He, too, burst into tears, for he was sad at heart that the dragon had carried off his wife, whom he had won at the risk of his life.

The princesses' three brothers were under enchantment too. One of them was in the castle, changed into the shape of a horse. One day the horse said to the sorrowing husband: "The dragon is away from home now. Let us go and steal the princess."

So they went to the dragon's castle, carried off the princess, and ran for home. The other brother of the three princesses was in the dragon's castle under enchantment in the shape of a horse.

When the dragon came home, he said to the horse: "Where is my princess?"

The horse answered: "They came and carried her away."

The dragon mounted the horse at once

and said : "Now we'll ride as fast as we can. We must overtake them."

The horse answered : "We cannot possibly overtake them."

But the dragon said : "Only let us start; we shall overtake them."

They started, and they overtook them near the castle. The dragon snapped the princess away at once, saying to the lad : "I promised to spare your life in return for that glass of water; now I have spared it, but don't dare to come to my castle ever again."

And with that the dragon rode home, carrying the princess with him.

Some time after that the horse said to the sorrowing husband : "The dragon is away from home again. Let us go and steal the princess."

So they went and stole her again.

The dragon came home and asked the horse : "Where is my princess?"

The horse answered : "Hibad! They have stolen her again, but we cannot overtake them this time."

The dragon said : "We must overtake them."

He mounted the horse, and they went

flying after them till at last they overtook
them. The dragon snapped away the princess, saying to the lad : " There's your life
spared for the second glass. But if you come
again, I'll tear you to pieces."

The lad was sorrowful, and wept and be-
wailed his fate because he had lost his wife
for ever. But the horse said :

" I will give you one more counsel. I
know a place where there are some young
ravens. We will go there, and you must take
the young ravens from their nest on the tree.
The old ones will fly at you and peck you—
they won't want to let you have their young
chicks ; but tell them that you won't give
them back their chicks unless they bring you
the healing water and the water of life.

" When they bring the water, take one
of the young ravens and pull its head off ;
then dip it in the healing water and put the
head to the body again. That's how you
will be certain that they have brought you
the real water of life. If the wound grows
together again, you may be sure it is the
real water of life. As soon as the wound
has grown together, take the water of life
and pour some of it into the raven's bill, and

when the bird revives, you will know quite
certainly that it is the water of life."

The lad did all this. The old ravens
brought him the water in leather bottles. He
took one of the chicks, pulled its head off,
dipped it into the healing water, and the
wound grew together again. Then he poured
some of the water of life into its bill, and
it came alive again. Then he put the young
ravens back into the nest again, took the water,
and went home.

When he got there, the horse said to him :
" The dragon is away from home to-day. Let
us go and see if we can get the princess."

So off they went and carried away the
princess. They ran off as fast as they could.

The dragon came home and asked the
horse : " Where is my princess ? "

The horse replied : " She's gone from us.
They've carried her off again, and this time
we shall never catch up with them."

The dragon said in a rage : " What should
prevent us from getting her back ? Let's go
at once."

So they flew after them, and they reached
the castle just as the fugitives were going
in through the gate.

The dragon snapped the princess away, saying to the lad: "You rascal! I told you I would tear you to pieces if you came a third time for her."

So he caught hold of him, and took a foot in each claw, and tore him in two. Then he went off with the princess and the horse.

The lad's horse took the healing water, dipped the two halves into it, put the one against the other, and they grew together. Then he took the water of life and poured it into the lad's mouth, and he was alive again. Then they went into the castle.

The lad was weeping bitterly and crying out that all was over, that now he would be separated from his wife for ever. But the horse gave him comfort, saying:

"Well, I really don't know what advice I ought to give you now. We have been three times, and he caught up with us every time. And the last time you were torn in pieces. I don't know how things will turn out. But I have another brother across the Red Sea, and he is stronger than I or the dragon. If we could only get him, we should be sure to kill the dragon. But it's a hard thing to do, for he is in service with the Devil's grandmother. We will try it together, if only we can manage to cross the Red Sea. And, if you follow the advice I give you, you will get the horse.

"You must serve the Devil's grandmother for three days, and, when you have served the three days, you must ask for that lean horse as wages. You will have to herd twelve horses for three days. Nobody has ever managed to do it yet. When the first day's service is done, on the next day the Devil's grandmother always cuts off the servant's head and hangs it on a hook. Now, listen carefully. While you are herding the horses, anything the hag gives you to eat at home, eat your fill of it. But, if she gives you anything to eat in the field, do not eat it, but throw it away. If you were to eat it, sleep would come down on you, your horses would stray, and the Devil's grandmother would cut off your head and hang it upon a hook."

So off they went together till they came to the Red Sea. As they were drawing near to the sea, they saw a huge fly entangled in a cobweb and struggling to free itself. So the lad went up to it and said : " Poor fly !

You can't get out of that cobweb; wait a bit, and I will help you."

The cobweb was as big as a sheet, but he tore it in two and the fly crept out.

The fly said: "Thank you for helping me out of the cobweb. Tear one of my feet from under my belly, and, whenever you are in need, think of me, and I will help you."

The lad thought: "Poor fly! how could you help me?" Nevertheless, he tore off one of her feet and kept it.

Then he went on his way, and he saw a wolf with his tail trapped under a heavy log, and he was unable to help himself, for wolves have stiff backs, and no wolf has ever been able to turn. The lad rolled the log away and released the wolf.

The wolf said: "Thank you for helping me. Take one of my claws, and, whenever you are in sore need, think of me, and I will help you." So the lad took one of his claws and kept it.

When he got quite close to the sea, he saw a crab as big as a barrel. The crab was lying on the sand with his belly upwards, and he couldn't manage to turn himself over again. So the lad went and turned the crab over again. The crab asked him where he was going. He said he was going to the Devil's grandmother across the Red Sea.

The crab said : " My dear lad, I'll make a bridge for you across the sea, so that you will be able to get across. But, besides that, you must pluck off one of my claws from under my belly, and when you are in sore need, think of me, and I will help you."

So he plucked off one of the claws and kept it. The crab sidled into the sea, and immediately all the crabs of the sea came together, and they closed in on one another so that they made a bridge across the sea. The lad crossed the bridge and came to the Devil's grandmother. She was standing waiting for him in the doorway of her house, and welcomed him. He'd just come at the right time ; she wanted him to herd her horses. She gave him plenty of good food to eat, and sent him out to the fields. She put twelve horses in his charge, and said to him :

" Look to it that you herd them well, for if you lose one of them you will lose your head. Just look here at these twenty-four posts, with a hook on each one of them. There are heads on twenty-three of them. The last hook is waiting for your head. If you herd my horses badly, that hook is waiting for your head."

Then she fitted him out for herding the horses. She gave him a piece of bread, so that he might have enough to eat and not starve. He meant to follow the horse's advice, and threw the bread away. But a fierce hunger came upon him, and he had to go and look for the bread and eat it up.

The moment he had eaten it he fell asleep and all the horses were lost. When he awoke there wasn't a single horse there. Sorrowfully he said: "The Devil's grandmother was right; my head will hang from that hook." In his grief he thought of the fly, and it came flying up and called out: "Why are you weeping and wailing?"

He said that he had been hungry, and had been forced to eat the bread, so that he fell asleep and all the horses were lost.

The fly tried to comfort him, saying: "Don't be troubled, dear lad; I will help you."

So she called together all the flies, and

they flew everywhere looking for the horses, and when they found them, they buzzed round them and plagued them till they drove them up to the herdsman. He drove them joyfully home.

The Devil's grandmother welcomed them, and when she saw that all the horses were there, she said : " You've herded them well enough, for you have brought them all back." Then she seized a hatchet and began to beat the horses with it, and most of all the lean one, till the flesh hung in strips from its body. The lad was sorry for the horse, for the hag was beating it hardest and it was the leanest of them all. But the Devil's grandmother took a salve and anointed the horses' wounds, and they were healed by morning.

The next day she fitted him out again for herding the horses, and gave him some more of the bread, telling him to eat it all. But when he came to the pasture he crumbled the bread and trampled the crumbs into the ground, so that it should be uneatable. But it was no good. He was forced to dig it up and eat it, earth and all, so great was the hunger that the Devil's grandmother had sent against him. In a moment he fell asleep and all the horses were lost.

When he woke he saw that there were no horses there. He wept and wailed. But he thought of the wolf, and the wolf came running up and asked him: "Why are you weeping and wailing? Don't be troubled; I will help you."

He went and summoned all the wolves. A great flock of wolves ran up, and they scattered everywhere, looking for the horses. When they found them, they drove them to the herdsman, each horse with a wolf at its side leading it by the ear. The herdsman was overjoyed, and took the horses and drove them home.

The Devil's grandmother was waiting for him in front of the house. She said: "Indeed you have herded them well; this is the second day that you have brought them all home." But she beat the horses with the hatchet far worse than the day before; then she anointed their wounds with the salve, so that they should be healed by morning.

On the third day she sent him out again to herd the horses, and gave him some more of the bread, telling him to eat it and not to throw it away. But when he came to the pasture he threw the bread down on the sand and trampled it in, so that it should be uneatable. But he had to search it out again, so great was the hunger the Devil's grandmother sent against him. The moment he had finished it he fell asleep and the horses were lost. When he woke he burst into tears. This time it was all up with him; the fly and the wolf had helped him before, but the crab had already made a bridge for him, so there was nobody to help him. The horses didn't know where to hide themselves to save themselves from being beaten by the Devil's grandmother, so they leapt into the sea, where nobody could find them.

The herdsman was in agony, and he kept on wailing that now his head must hang upon that hook. At last he thought of the crab. The crab turned round in the sea, and instantly all the crabs collected and began searching the sea for the horses, and they pinched them until they drove them out of the sea. But the lean one, since he couldn't think of a better hiding-place, crouched under the crab's belly. The other crabs set to work to look for him, and at last they found him. The big crab had to turn over, and then they drove the lean horse out. The herdsman took the horses and drove them home joyfully, because his three days of service were now over.

The Devil's grandmother was waiting for him, and she beat the horses with the hatchet so fiercely that their flesh hung in strips from their bodies. Then she anointed them with the salve, and the wounds healed by morning. In the morning she asked the herdsman what wages he wanted. He answered: " I want nothing but that lean old horse."

She said: " It would be a sorry thing to give you such a wretched horse in return for such good service; I will give you the best horse."

He answered: " I won't take any horse but the lean one."

She asked him why he wanted the leanest one. He replied: " Because I am sorry for him, for he always gets the worst beating. I will have that one, and no other."

So she said: " Well, I will give him to you, if you must have him, but I will give you this fat one too. You can ride on his back home and lead the lean one with you."

He mounted the fat horse and rode off. But when they were drawing near to the gate, the lean horse said : "Get down from that horse and mount me, or you will be the worse for it."

So he jumped down from the fat horse and mounted the lean one.

The fat horse growled : "It's the Devil gave you that advice."

And the lean horse said : "If you had gone under the gate on that horse's back, he would have dashed you against the vault of the gate, so that your head would have been knocked off, and you would have been killed."

So they came safely home. When the princesses saw him come back they were delighted.

The other horse said : "Now, brother, let us go. The dragon is away from home, and the princess will be ours." So they went and carried off the princess.

When the dragon came home, he asked his horse : "Where is my princess ?"

The horse replied : "She has gone, and

this time we shan't get her back. The horse
from the Red Sea has come, and he will
get the better of us all."

The dragon took no heed of that, but flew
after them and caught them up just by the
gate. He was going to snap the princess
away, but this time he could not do it. For
the horse from over the Red Sea kicked his
nose with his hoof, so that the dragon fell
down from his horse, and the other two
horses fell upon him, and between them they
killed the dragon.

They came to the castle with the princess,
and they were congratulating one another on
their victory over their enemy. Then the
horse which had been giving good advice
to his rider all the time said: " Now, dear
brother-in-law, take my sword there hanging
from the ceiling and cut my head off."

He was sad and said : " How could I do
that, after all the acts of kindness you have
done for me ? "

The horse said : " My good friend, I cannot
tell you why you must behead me, but you
would do me a great wrong if you did not
do it."

So he hesitated no longer, but cut his head

off. The blood spurted up twelve feet high, and instantly the horse became a beautiful youth. Seeing that, the lad was quick to behead the other horses, and they all turned into handsome princes like the first one.

They all thanked him for delivering them, and they made him king of that castle, and there he lived with his wife and her two sisters in all happiness and harmony till they died. The three brothers took possession of the dragon's castle.

THE BEAR, THE EAGLE, AND THE FISH

ONCE there was a count and he had three daughters. All of them were young and as pretty as peacocks, but the youngest was the loveliest of them all. The count had little money to spend, for he had lost it all by gambling. And so—since he had to spend the time in some way or other—he used to go hunting. One day when he was out hunting he lost his way in a forest, and he could not find his way out of it. Suddenly a big bear rushed out at him, shouting at the top of his voice. He said he would show him the way out of the forest and, besides, he would give him as much gold and silver as he wanted on one condition, and that condition was that the count should give him one of his daughters in marriage. The count was terrified. But after thinking it over for a time, he consented at last. The bear showed him the way out of the forest and gave him everything he had promised, and so the count was pleased.

He spent his time eating and drinking and gambling, till all the money melted away. He never so much as gave a thought to the bear, until one day, when the eldest daughter was marriageable, a carriage came rolling up. The carriage was drawn by a pair of raven-black horses, and in it sat a prince with cheeks of white and red, whose robes blazed with gold. He came and took the eldest daughter and drove off. The countess wept, but the count did not mind a bit, but being short of money, he began hunting again.

One day he lost his way again, and this time an eagle flew down to him and promised to show him the way out of the forest, and to give him heaps of money into the bargain, if he would only give him his second daughter in return. The bargain was made and the eagle fetched away the second daughter, and only the youngest was left at home. Yet even her the count sold, and it was a fish that got her.

So the count and the countess were left alone. They were very sad, but after a time a boy was born to them, and they watched

over him like the apple of their eye. When
the boy was grown up, he saw that the
countess looked sad sometimes, and he gave
her no rest till she had told him everything.
When he had heard the story, he put his
best clothes on, took his sword, mounted his
horse, and said good-bye to his parents, telling
them that he was going to search for his lost
sisters.

So he rode on till he came to the eldest
sister. Her he found playing with three little
bear cubs, for these were her babies. He met
his brother-in-law, who gave him three hairs
and told him to rub those hairs with his
fingers if he found himself in any difficulty.
Then he went to the second sister, and found
her with two eaglets and the old eagle, his
brother-in-law, as well. The eagle gave him
three feathers, saying they would be of help
to him in time of need. He thanked the eagle
for that and went on his way, and at last he
came to his youngest sister. It was not so
easy to get to her, for she dwelt under the
water, and he had to drop into her house
through the chimney. He would have missed
the chimney if it hadn't been for the smoke
from it: it was bluish smoke, hardly visible.

His sister welcomed him heartily and showed him her baby, a pretty little fish, and her husband, a giant fish. The lad got three fish-scales from the husband to use in time of trouble.

He learned that the bear and the eagle were the brothers of the fish. They were sons of a powerful king, but they had been enchanted by an envious magician and turned into these shapes. The sorcerer could take different forms. But the brother must not let that dismay him. He must get hold of a golden egg which was hidden in the sorcerer and throw it on the ground. If he began to grow faint and did not know what to do, he must call one of his brothers-in-law, and he would advise him what to do.

And so it was. The young count attacked the magician, who turned into a bull. But the young count was not afraid: he rubbed the bear's hair; the bear came running up and tore the bull in pieces. But out of the bull flew a wild duck and tried to escape. Then the count thought of the eagle feathers, and immediately the eagle flew up, and he tore the duck to pieces. But a golden egg fell from the duck and it rolled into the pond. But that

too was of no avail, for the count rubbed the
fish scales, and after a while the fish threw the
egg upon the bank.   The count caught it and
flung it to the ground so that it was smashed
into many pieces.

At once all around was changed.   The pond
turned into a meadow upon which a beautiful
castle was shining.   The castle was full of
servants and the three princes, with their wives
and children, were just walking out of it.   All
were overjoyed to be so happily delivered,
and, when they had enough of rejoicing, they
started off to find their parents.

Their first journey was to the old count and
countess, so that they might enjoy the sight of
their children and grandchildren.   Afterwards
they hastened to the old king.   He ordered
many cannon to be fired, and prepared a
splendid banquet.   And he gave the kingdom
to his eldest son.   The second son went to the
land of the count, and it was divided between
him and his brother-in-law.   And the youngest
went to the disenchanted castle.   All of them
reigned prosperously and wisely in their
several realms and, if they haven't died since,
they are reigning still.

KOJATA

ONCE there was a king who had an only son. One day the king went to inspect his estates. He came to the first farm and found it all right. Before he had finished going the round of his estates, thirteen big farms in all, he forgot that his wife was about to have a child. On his way home he came to a forest, and such a thirst came upon him that he bade his driver stop and look for some water. The driver looked everywhere for water, but he couldn't find any. So the king himself went to look for it, and he found a well.

Now, just as he was going to drink, he kneeled down and he saw something in the well which had claws like a crab and red eyes. It seized him by the beard with one of its claws—he had a pretty long beard— and it refused to let him go unless he promised to give it the thing that he had at home unknown to himself. So he said to himself: "I know everything at home." But he forgot about his wife's condition. By this time his wife had been delivered of a prince, and so the king, without knowing it, had promised his son to the thing in the well. And on that it let him go.

When he got home he saw the new-born prince, and of course he was very sad. He remained so for twelve years. The prince asked him why he was so sad. And the king answered: "Because you are sold." The prince told him not to worry about it; he would be able to help himself.

The prince called for his horse and started out. He had been riding five days' journey from his home, when he came to a lake. There he tethered his horse. He saw thirteen ducks swimming on the lake, and there were thirteen shifts lying on the bank. So he carried off one of the shifts and hid himself. When they saw this, twelve of the ducks flew away, but the thirteenth was running hither and thither, looking for her shift. So when he saw her running hither and thither looking for her shift, he came out of his hiding-place. Now the father of those ducks was the being which had seized the king by the beard. He was a sorcerer, and his name was Kojata.

This girl was his youngest daughter. And she said to the prince:

"Now I will give you a good counsel. You will save me and I will save you. My father will set you a difficult task. I will perform it for you, but you must not let him know that I am helping you. Leave your horse here and hurry on to my father's. He will give you a lodging, and he will give you three days to consider over the task. You will be in your room alone, and in the evening I will come humming to your window, for I shall come to you in a bee's shape, because I can't come in any other way. And you must follow my advice. My father has thirteen daughters, and we all resemble one another exactly and we all wear the same sort of clothes. You will have to find out which is the youngest, but you will have no other means of recognizing me than by noticing a tiny fly under my left eye, so be very careful about it."

So it was. The sorcerer called him in and the thirteen daughters were standing

in a row. The sorcerer asked him whether
he could make out which was the youngest;
if he could do so, his life would be spared.
So he went the round of them three times,
but it was as much as he could do to recognize her. But he pointed her out. She
was the third from the end. So the sorcerer
asked him who had been giving him advice.
But the prince answered that it was none
of his business.

The next day the sorcerer gave him
another task: to build a palace of pure gold
and silver without using hammer or trowel.
The prince was very worried about it. But
in the evening the youngest daughter came
flying to him again, and she gave him a
wand. At a single stroke of the wand the
palace rose up ready-built, and it was more
perfect than the old one. In the morning
he was strolling about the palace looking
round him. When King Kojata saw him,
he came up to him and stopped: "Who
has given you this counsel?" he asked.
The prince answered that it was the person
who had given him advice the time before.

So the sorcerer set him the third task,
and this time the daughter was not able to

advise him. She came to him in the evening and said : "I have no other advice than for both of us to flee at once, otherwise you will be lost and I too."

Now, in the evening she turned herself into a horse, and he mounted her and rode as far as the lake. There he found his own horse, and they both mounted it and rode off at full speed. Soon she heard a great noise behind her, so she turned herself into a church and the prince became a monk. The sorcerer's apprentices were riding in pursuit of them. When they got as far as the church they turned and went back to Kojata. When they came to him they said that they had not overtaken anybody ; they had only seen a church and a monk in it. And he said : " Those were they ! "

Next day he sent them again to pursue the runaways. Though they were riding faster than the day before, again they heard a trampling behind them. So she turned herself into a great river and him into an old broken bridge. Their pursuers came as far as the river and the bridge, and then they turned back and reported to their king, Kojata, that they had seen nothing but a

river and a bridge. He said at once:
"Well, those were they!"

On the third day the runaways started
again and made for the border as fast as
they could, and soon they were in their own
land. When they reached the third church,
the sorcerer had no more power over them.
He began to tear his hair and knock his
head against the ground and to curse his
daughter for tricking him.

So the young king came home, bringing
a lovely young princess with him. His
father was very pleased at that!

109

SHEPHERD HYNEK

To cut a long story short, there was a prince and he had three sons. The first two followed in their father's footsteps, but the third did not. He said he would like to be a forester. The father was angry and turned him out of the house. What was he to do with the fellow, when he was so obstinate and would be a forester?

"Well, be whatever you like," said the prince, and he gave him a shepherd's dress and Hynek went out into the world.

He had been walking through a forest for three days. He was hungry and cold, and everything seemed to be against him. He was tired too, and at last he fell asleep under a tree. As he was sleeping, a black man came to him. He would not leave him to sleep, but waked him up. Hynek was frightened. But he told him there was no need to be afraid. He was a good man, though his skin was black. So Hynek stayed with him for seven years and learnt the seven languages, zither playing, and all that sort of thing.

Now the seven years were over. In that land there was a king who had an only daughter. And there was a fierce dragon which was ravaging the whole of that kingdom, and everybody was forced to give him one sheep and one human being to appease him. So the lot fell upon the princess too. The black man told Hynek that something ought to be done to deliver the people and to save the princess from being devoured by that dragon.

" Go to the next homestead," he said, " and ask to be taken on as a shepherd, and in the morning you will have to drive the sheep into this forest."

So they took leave of one another. Hynek was engaged as shepherd, and in the morning he drove the sheep into the forest, where the black man was waiting for him. When he came with the sheep, the black man gave him a wand and a ring, and said :

" When you turn this ring, you will be brought to a castle where a giant dwells, and you will have to tackle the giant. This wand will help you to do it. Then you must take his robe, his horse, and his sword. Then you will be brought to the town, and it will be about the time that the princess will be brought out."

So Hynek took his leave and found everything just as he had said. As he came near to the castle, the giant was looking out and said :

"You earthworm, what are you looking for?"

"Oh! I should like to have a try for that big head of yours."

The giant fell into a rage. He was holding a great club in his hand, and he flung it at Hynek, but Hynek dodged aside and the club sank deep into the ground, it had been flung with such force. So Hynek went right up to him, and, crack! he struck him with the wand. So the giant tumbled over. Hynek took his sword and struck his head off. Then he took an iron key out of the giant's pocket. He opened the lock, took the robe and the horse, and dressed himself as became a knight. Then he turned the ring, and in a moment he found himself on the road along which they were bringing the princess to be devoured by the dragon. When he saw the procession, he asked :

" What's going on here, and why are the people in such grief ? "

" Because the princess is to be devoured by a dragon to-day."

Hynek said : " For the sake of her beauty, show me his den where he dwells."

So he rode up to the rock and called out loudly : " Now, dragon, come on ; your meal is ready here, waiting for you."

But the dragon answered : " I don't want it to-day ; come to-morrow, at eleven."

So Hynek returned. He rode towards them and said that the dragon would not leave his den to-day. So they all went back to the town with the knight, and the king would not let him go away on any account. But Hynek began to make excuses. He had to deliver a letter for the field mar-shal and he could not remain there. Then he turned the ring on his finger, and instantly he was in the castle again. He left the clothes and the horse there, putting the clothes tidily together. Then he put on his shepherd's dress, turned the ring, and at once he was near the forest, where the black man had been tending his sheep meanwhile. He greeted him kindly :

"You have done everything well. Always act like that."

So he drove the sheep home and played the zither again. Everybody ran up to the door to listen to the magic playing of the shepherd. But he said nothing to anybody.

The next day he drove the sheep to the forest still earlier. The black man was there waiting for him, and said : " Follow my advice and you will be happy."

He said that he would do so. The black man was to mind the sheep again. He gave Hynek the wand and the ring, and Hynek came to another castle.

The giant was looking out as he came up ; he was standing in the doorway. He asked the lad grimly what he was looking for.

"Oh ! it's nothing. I only want to try for that big head of yours."

The giant was holding a hammer and he hurled it at him. No eye could see where it fell. Hynek leapt towards him, and, crack ! he struck him with the wand, and the giant fell over and Hynek cut his head off too. He

took a silver key out of the giant's pocket
and went straight to the castle. There he
chose a robe, girded on a sword, took a horse,
and turned the ring again. Once more he
was on the road where the princess was being
brought to be devoured. He asked them in
a different language why they were wailing so.

"Well, our princess is to be devoured by
the dragon to-day. He would not leave his
den yesterday."

"Show me his den: I will sacrifice myself
for the sake of her beauty."

They showed him the rock, and he rode
straight up to it and called out: " Now, dragon,
come on; your meal is ready here."

" I don't want it to-day, wait till eleven
to-morrow."

The king was still less willing to let him
go this time, but he found some excuse, turned
his horse, and went back with everything to
the castle.

Then he returned to the forest and the
black man. The black man said: " Drive
your sheep home now, but come earlier to-
morrow, for a heavy task awaits you."

Hynek could not rest that night: he was
so afraid that he would be too late. As soon

as dawn came he let out the flock and drove it to the forest. When he got there, the black man said to him : " There's only to-day now. It will be the last time. But it will be a heavy task for you to tackle the third giant and the dragon." Then he gave him the wand and the ring, and said that the key to-day would be of gold. He must choose the robe and take a black horse, and he must take with him the sword with which he had killed the giant and the dragon.

He turned the ring and was brought to the third castle. Here was a giant again, much huger than the other two. He ran at Hynek, but, crack ! Hynek struck him with the wand. Then he took his sword and killed him. Then he opened the castle with a golden key ; he went to the stable, then he put on a green robe and brought out a black horse. There was a sword hanging there, and he girded it on. Then he turned the ring, and in a moment he was on the road along which they were bringing the princess to be devoured by the dragon.

He asked them in yet another language why they were so sorrowful. He was ready to sacrifice himself for the sake of her beauty.

So they showed him the den in which the
dragon dwelt, and he called out: "Well, come
on, dragon; your meal is ready and waiting
for you here."

Now the rock began to shake; all the stones
came rolling down, and the dragon flew out
of the rock, his seven heads burning with
flame, and he made straight for Hynek.
Hynek began cutting at the seven heads until
he was weary that he could not do any more.
Then the horse began to crush the dragon,
until after a while Hynek, being rested, took
his sword, and at once he cut all the seven
heads off.

He was so scorched by the fire that he
could not run away, and he fainted on the spot.
The people had seen what was happening, so
they rode up and carried him away, lest he
should perish of the dragon's poison. They
brought him and laid him in the princess's
lap. She gave him her ring and a golden
neckchain, and so he recovered his senses
and found himself lying in the princess's lap.
He was afraid that he had stayed too long,
for he was supposed to be with the marshal
by this time. They were all trying to hold
him back from going, but he found an excuse

and promised he would come back within three days. So at last they just had to let him go.

He returned to the castle, where he put everything back in its place again, except the sword, which he took with him and gave to the black man. The black man said to him: " You have succeeded now, and it will be well with both of us."

So Hynek drove his sheep home rejoicing. He was playing the zither, and all the people gathered outside to listen to his rare and sweet music. He asked what had happened to the princess : had the dragon devoured her?

" Oh no ! A knight delivered her, and the king is going to give her in marriage to him."

"Alas! silly shepherd that I am, why did I not tackle him myself with my shepherd's staff ! "

But they all laughed at him : " You mind your sheep, that's what befits you."

In the royal castle the wedding-feast was ready. The sixth day had come and they were still waiting for him. But the bridegroom did not come and the princess was sad. On the sixth day he asked the marshal if he

could go to the castle to play his zither to the
princess; he would like to cheer her, since she
was so sad.

"You may go, and, if you succeed, you
shall make some extra money."

So Hynek went and played, and the music
was so sweet that the lords could listen to
nothing but his beautiful playing. He played
for three hours, and then he must go home.
They asked him what reward he would like.

"Nothing but to drink a cup of wine with
the princess."

He had ready the ring which the princess
had given him when he was in her lap. His
request was granted, and the rest of the
musicians who were there were angry with him
for claiming so insignificant a reward. When
they had filled the cup for him, he drank the
wine and dropped the ring into the cup.

Now, the cupbearer who was filling the cup
looked into it and saw the glittering ring. So
he hastened to the princess with it. She
recognized it as her own, so she ordered them
to bring that shepherd before her.

"Well," he said, "surely they won't beat
me!"

They brought him before the princess, and

she made him tell her how he had got that
ring and how he had been clothed.

So he said: "All those three days I was
with you."

Hynek did not go back to the marshal,
though he complained of the loss of his shepherd. He was clad in royal robes now, and
they had a splendid wedding in the castle.
But the princess did not know what his parent-
age was, although she could see that he was
not a low-born man.

So after a year he said he would like to
visit his parents, and he told her to prepare
for the journey. She was to send a letter to
Prince So-and-So that the young queen was
going to visit him. He would go on ahead.

So he put his shepherd's dress on once more
and purposely tore it in several places, and,
when his princess arrived and everybody was
welcoming her, he went straight into the great
hall. Now, when the old Prince saw that it
was his son all tattered and torn, he bade them
put him under lock and key. But he had
no difficulty in escaping, and while they were
feasting, he came into the hall again and sat
down next to the princess. The father was
furious that his son should behave so shame-

fully. But the princess reassured him. It was all right, she said. She did not mind at all; he might sit where he pleased.

After dinner she called for a bath. They prepared it for her. But Hynek was quicker, and slipped into the bathroom before her. She shut the door and he put on his royal robes, and then they went before his father. The Prince was frightened, since he had thought so ill of his son, and he fell on his knees. But Hynek lifted him up and himself kneeled before him and asked his forgiveness.

Then came in the black man. He gave Hynek the sword and bade him cut his head off. Hynek would not repay his kindness in this way.

" Then we shall both be unhappy."

So when he saw what he was to do, he cut the head off and, when he had done that, an English prince appeared in his stead. He was only eighteen years old. All his followers woke up too. Hynek accompanied him to England, and then took leave of him.

How are they all now?

I don't know.

THE THREE ROSES

ONCE upon a time there was a mother who had three daughters. There was to be a market in the next town, and she said she would go to it. She asked the daughters what she should bring them back. Two of them named a great number of things; she must buy all of them, they said. You know the sort of women, and the sort of things they would want. Well, when they had asked for more than enough, the mother asked the third daughter:

" And you, don't you want anything ? "

"No, I don't want anything; but, if you like, you can bring me three roses, please."

If she wanted no more than that, her mother was ready to bring them.

When the mother knew all she wanted, she went off to market. She bought all she could, piled it all on her back, and started for home. But she was overtaken by nightfall, and the poor mother completely lost her way and could go no farther. She wandered through the forest till she was quite worn out, and at last she came to a palace, though she had never before heard of any palace there. There was a large garden full of roses, so beautiful that no painter alive could paint them, and all the roses were smiling at her. So she remembered her youngest daughter, who had wished for just such roses. She had forgotten it entirely till then. Surely that was because she was so old! Now she thought: "There are plenty of roses here, so I will take these three."

So she went into the garden and took the roses. At once a basilisk came and demanded her daughter in exchange for the roses. The mother was terrified and wanted to throw the flowers away. But the basilisk said that wouldn't be any use, and he threatened to tear her to pieces. So she had to promise him her daughter. There was no help for it, and so she went home.

She took the three roses to her daughter and said: "Here are the roses, but I had to pay dearly for them. You must go to yonder castle in payment for them, and I don't even know whether you will ever come back."

But Mary seemed as though she didn't mind at all, and she said she would go. So the mother took her to the castle. There was everything she wanted there. Soon the basilisk appeared and told Mary that she must nurse him in her lap for three hours every day. There was no way out, do it she must, and so the basilisk came and she nursed him for three hours. Then he went out, but he came next day and the day after that. On the third day he brought a sword and told poor Mary to cut his head off.

She protested that she wasn't used to doing things like that, and do it she could not. But the basilisk said in a rage that, if that was so, he would tear her to pieces. As there was no choice, she went up to him and cut his head off. And as the basilisk's head rolled on the ground, there came forth from his body a long serpent, hissing horribly. He asked her to cut his head off again. Mary did not hesitate this time, but cut his head off at once.

The serpent (by the way, he held the golden keys of that palace in his mouth) was immediately changed into a beautiful youth, and he said in a pleasant voice: "This castle belongs to me, and, as you have delivered me, there is no help for it : I must marry you."

So there was a great wedding, the castle was full of their attendants, and they all had to play and dance. But the floor was of paper, so I fell through it, and here I am now.

127

THE ENCHANTED PRINCESSES

In the days of King Bambita, his two noble daughters oppressed the people, laying heavy taxes on them without the king's knowledge. The people cursed them, and the curses did their work. The princesses vanished. The king sent some of his servants to look for the princesses. But the servants came back empty-handed. None of them had been able to find the princesses.

Now, a captain and a lieutenant heard of the king's trouble. So the lieutenant went to the king, and "I see," says he, "that you are in trouble. I will go and look for the princesses."

"How much do you want for it?" asked the king.

"Twenty pounds."

The king agreed, and gave him the money. "If you find them," said he, "half of my kingdom is yours."

The lieutenant and the captain had plenty of money now, so they went to an inn and passed the time drinking. On the third day the captain said : " To-day I will go to the king. If he gave you twenty pounds, he is certain to give me more."

So he went to the king and said : " I see that your majesty is in trouble. I should like to go and look for the princesses.",

" How much do you want for it? " said the king.

" Thirty pounds."

Well, the king gave him the money without any more ado, adding that, if he found the princesses, he would get half of his kingdom.

They fell to drinking again and had a splendid time.

There was a drummer near them, and he heard them saying that they were to look for the princesses. So he went to the king and said : " I hear that your majesty is prostrated by sore trouble. I, too, would like to look for the princesses."

" How much do you want for it? "

" Forty pounds, at least."

The king gave him the money without

more ado.   The two officers and the drummer
left that inn for another, and so they went
on spending their money recklessly in one
drinking-house after another.   The drummer
went with the other two, but he was more
careful than they were.   He was not such
a spendthrift as the two officers.

They asked him where he meant to go.

"Wherever you go, I will go too," he
replied.

"Then why don't you join us and lead a
gay life?"

"That I can't do until I know where to
find the princesses."

They invited him to join them, but he
refused to do it.

At last they bought some bread and other
food, and they all set out together on their
journey.   They came to a dark forest, and
for a fortnight they searched it through and
through, but they could find nothing.   They
couldn't find their way out of the forest either,
so they agreed that one of them should climb
to the top of the highest tree to see which
way they ought to go.   The drummer, being
the youngest, climbed up a pine-tree.   He
called out :

"I can see a cottage. Look, I will throw my hat towards it, and do you follow the hat."

Well, they went on until they reached the cottage.

"Go into the room," says the drummer.

"After you," said both the officers at once.

So the drummer stepped inside, and an old crone welcomed him.

"Welcome, Drummer Anthony," said she. "How did you get here?"

"I have come to deliver the princesses, and only for that."

"Well, you will find them, but those other two fellows will get them from you by a trick."

She gave him a rope three hundred fathoms long and told him to bind it round his body. She also gave him some wine and a sponge. Then she said: "Not far from here there is a well. When you come to it, you must say that you will let yourself down into the well, if the other fellows will drink the fountain dry."

When they got to the well, the captain and the lieutenant began to drink the fountain, but it was just as full as before.

" If we kept on drinking this fountain till doomsday," they said, "we could not drink it dry."

So the drummer took the sponge, and at once the water began to disappear, and soon the well was dry. They began to quarrel as to who should go down the well. The one on the right side said the other ought to go, but at last they agreed that the drummer, who was the lightest, should go.

So he went down, and, when he reached the bottom of the well, he found a stone there. He drew it aside, and then he saw the light of the other world. He lowered himself on the rope into the other world. There he saw a beautiful palace. He went towards it. When he reached it, he saw that the table was laid for two persons. He ate his meal and then went into the second room. There he laid himself down to sleep, and when he awoke in the morning, he found the Princess Anne in the third room.

" Welcome," she said ; " what has brought you here ? "

He told her that he had come to deliver her.

She said : " I don't know whether you will

succeed in that.   Here is a sword ; see if you can brandish it."

The drummer took hold of the sword, but he could not even lift it, it was so heavy.

Then the princess gave him a ring.   "Take this," she said, "and whenever you think of me, you will become strong.   I have to hold the dragon in my lap for a whole hour.   As soon as he comes, he will smell a man. But you must cut him in two, for then I shall be delivered.   Just at nine o'clock he comes."

Just at nine o'clock the palace began to tremble and the dragon came in.   But the drummer encountered him and struck him in two with the sword.

After that the princess took him into another room.   "Now you have delivered me," she said.   "But my sister is in worse trouble still.   She has to hold a dragon in her lap for two hours, and that dragon is even stronger than this one."

Then they went into the fourth room, where was the Princess Antonia.   She, too, greeted him, and told him that he would be able to deliver her if he could brandish the sword beside her.   He tried, but he could

not even move it.   Then she gave him a
ring and told him that, whenever he thought
of her, he would have the strength of two
hundred men.   She said, too, that if he
succeeded in setting her free she would marry
him.

Soon eleven o'clock came.   The hall began
to tremble and the dragon appeared.   But, as
he was coming in, Anthony was ready for him
near the door, and he managed to cut the
dragon in two.

Now, when the two princesses had been set
free, they gathered all the precious stones they
could to take with them, and went to the
opening that led into the world.   But the
drummer had quite forgotten the old crone's
warning about the other two fellows, and he
sent the princesses up before him.   Each of
the officers took a princess for himself, and
the drummer was left behind at the bottom
of the well.   When his turn came, he was
careful enough to tie a stone to the rope.
His companions on the top pulled it up a
little way and then suddenly let it drop, throw-
ing down other stones into the well to kill
the drummer.   But he had remembered the
crone's warning that his friends would try to

trick him. So he jumped aside and remained there in the other world.

He went back to the palace and entered the seventh room. On the table were three boxes. He opened the first and found a whistle inside it. He blew the whistle, and in came some generals and asked what was his majesty's will. He said he had only whistled to find out if they were attending to their duty. Then he looked into the second box, and there he saw a bugle. He blew the bugle, and in came some officers, who said just what the generals had said. In the third box he found a drum. He beat the drum, and immediately he was surrounded by infantry and cavalry, a great multitude of soldiers. He asked whether any of them had ever been in Europe. Two men were found among them who had been shipwrecked.

"Where is the ship?" said the drummer.

"Here on the seacoast," they replied.

At that, Anthony decked himself out in a royal robe and started on his travels for Europe.

Meanwhile the two princesses had reached home. One was engaged to be married to the lieutenant, the other to the captain.

But when the time for the wedding came, both the princesses, still thinking of Anthony, asked for a delay of one year, and their royal father granted their request.

Anthony arrived safely in that land. He met a traveller and said to him, " Look here, why should you not change clothes with me ? "

He was glad to do so, and Anthony went on to the town in which the princesses lived and sought out a goldsmith. He asked the goldsmith for work.

" I haven't work enough for myself," said the goldsmith.

" Well," said the drummer, " I have had an order for two rings, although I was only walking the street."

" You are a lucky fellow," said the goldsmith, and his wife, when she heard of it, spoke in the drummer's favour, so he was taken on as assistant.

" Now," said he, " give me what I want and I will make the rings. But nobody must enter my room : I will take my meals in at the door."

On the third day one ring was finished, and this one was meant for the Princess Anne.

"You must take this ring to the Princess Anne, master," said he.

"So I will," said the goldsmith; "but what is your price for it?"

"A thousand pounds," said he.

"If that's so, I won't go. They would put me in jail."

"Be easy," said Anthony, "nothing will happen to you."

So the goldsmith went to the palace, and sent in a message that his assistant had made a ring for the Princess Anne. She sent a message that she had not ordered a ring, but she would look at it. As soon as she saw it, she asked: "How much do you want for this?" He replied that he was almost afraid to say that it was worth a thousand pounds.

"Oh! it is worth much more than that," she said, and she paid the sum at once.

The goldsmith returned home and told his wife what he had got for the ring. She wondered what sort of person their new assistant was. The master brought the money to him, but the assistant would not accept it.

"You can keep the money for yourself," he said, "and I have just finished the ring for

the Princess Antonia. You will have to go
to the palace again with this."

This time the master-goldsmith was ready
enough to go. " How much am I to ask for
this ring ? " he said.

"Ask two thousand pounds."

So he was brought to the princess, and he
told her that his apprentice had made a ring
for her. She answered that she had not
ordered a ring. " However, show it to me."

As soon as she glanced at it, she said:
" How much do you want for this ? "

" Two thousand pounds."

" Oh ! it's worth much more than that,"
she said.

So she paid down the money and told the
master-goldsmith to fetch his assistant to her.
As soon as the master came home, he told
his wife everything. She was still more
astonished.

" O Lord ! " she said, " I cannot understand
it at all."

The master told Anthony that the princess
bade him come and see her.

" She can come to me," was his reply.

When the princess heard that, she lost no
time, but took some royal garments for him,

and drove to Anthony's house in the royal coach. She went straight to him and said, "I am come to bring you home with me, Anthony."

She bade him put on the royal robe she had brought with her for him, and they drove together to the palace, and their marriage was celebrated not long after.

The two officers thought the king would banish them or inflict some punishment upon them, but he pardoned them and gave them sufficient money to live at the court. Anthony himself did not care for royalty. He and his wife arranged that they would return to the place where he had first found the princesses. So they departed for that land, but a storm drove them on shore near to the place where he had met the old crone. She gave him welcome.

" So you are back again," she said.

They explained to her that what they wished was to go back to that palace beneath the fountain.

"Well," she said, "I will show you the way to the other world, and I will let you down the well."

They came to the opening, and Anthony

was about to enter the well, but the old hag begged him to wait with her and let the princess go on before.

So the princess was let down to the bottom of the well, and then the crone said : "I won't let you follow her unless you first cut off my head."

"This is a strange way to repay the good you have done me," said Anthony.

"Well, unless you promise this you will never see your princess again."

So he had to promise, and with that she waved her wand and a road appeared, which led them straight to the princess. Then Anthony struck off the crone's head, and they found themselves amid crowds of farmers who were ploughing and soldiers standing at attention, and one and all welcoming their new lords. For this land was an enchanted land, and the old crone was a witch.

THE TWIN BROTHERS

ONCE there was a princess, and she was under a curse and enchantment, so that she had to spend her life in the shape of a fish. One day a woman happened to be working in the meadow by the river, and she saw a flock of birds flying above the river and talking to the fish. The woman wondered what it was that was there, so she went to the waterside and looked in. All she saw was a fish swimming about. So she said : "I should like to eat you, fish. I feel sure you would do me good."

Now, when she said that, the fish answered : "You could save me. You will have twin sons, although you have never had any children before."

The woman said that, if she could help her in that, there was nothing the fish could ask that she would not do to deliver her.

The fish answered : " Catch me and take me

to your field. There you must bury me and plant a rose-tree over me. When the roses first come into bloom you will bear twin sons. After three years, dig in the place where you buried me and you will find two swords, and these you must keep. Your mare will have two foals and your bitch will have two pups, and each of your twins will have a sword, a horse, and a dog. Those swords will have the virtue that they will help your sons to victory over everybody. I shall be delivered as soon as my body has rotted."

When the twin sons grew up they were very clever, and so they said : "We must try our luck in the world. We are bold enough. One of us will go to the East and one to the West. Each of us must look at his sword every morning to see if the other needs his help. For the sword will begin to rust as soon as one of us is in peril."

So they cast lots which way they should go, and each of them took his sword, his horse, and his dog, and away they went.

The first rode through deep forests, and he met a fierce dragon and a lion ; so he attacked the dragon, which had nine heads. The lion stayed quiet while the knight attacked the dragon, and at last he succeeded in cutting one of the dragon's heads off. He felt tired then, and the lion took his place; then the knight cut two more heads off the dragon. And so it went on till he had all the heads cut off. Then he cut out the tongues from all the nine heads and kept them, and so went forward on his adventurous journey.

Now, it chanced that there were some wood-cutters in these forests, and one of them collected all the dragon's heads, having come across them by chance. That dragon used to come to the town and devour one person every visit. This time the lot had fallen upon the princess, and so she was to be devoured by the dragon. So the town was all hung with black cloth. The woodcutter knew all about this, so he went with the heads to the town to sue for the princess, for it had been proclaimed that whoever killed the dragon should be her husband. When the princess saw that such a low-born man was to be her husband she was taken aback, and tried by all the means in her power to delay the wedding.

The knight happened to come to the town just then, and he saw a good inn, so he rode up to it. The innkeeper came at once to ask what he could do for him. Now, there were other guests there, and it was a busy place. The guests were all talking of the one matter : when the princess was going to marry the man who had killed the dragon. The wedding ought to have been long ago, but the bride and her parents kept putting it off. The knight listened to all this talk, and then he asked :

"Are you sure that it was that woodcutter who killed the dragon ? "

They answered that it certainly was, for the heads were preserved in the palace.

The knight said nothing, but when he thought the proper time had come he rode to the palace. The princess saw him from the window, and she wondered who it might be. He was ushered in, and he went straight to the princess and told her everything. He asked her whether he might attend the wedding.

She answered: " I am not at all pleased with my marriage. I would much rather marry you, sir."

He asked her why.

" If he killed the dragon he must be a great man."

"He is such a low-born man," said she, "that it is not likely that he killed the dragon."

"I should like to see him," said he.

So they brought the woodcutter before him, and the knight asked to see the heads. So they brought the heads. He looked at the heads and said:

"There are no tongues in these heads. Where are the tongues?"

Then he turned to the woodcutter: "Did you really kill the cruel dragon?" he said.

The woodcutter persisted in his story.

"And how did you cut the heads off?"

"With my hatchet."

"Why, you couldn't do it with your hatchet. You are a liar."

The woodcutter was taken aback and did not know what to say. He was frightened already, but he said: "It happened that the dragon didn't have any tongues."

The knight produced the tongues and said: "Here are the tongues, and it was I who killed the cruel dragon."

The princess took hold of him and embraced and kissed him, and she was ready to marry him on the spot. As for the woodcutter, he was kicked out in disgrace, and they put him into jail for some time too. So the princess married the knight and they lived happily together.

One day, looking out of the window, he saw in the distance, among the mountains, a black castle. He asked his wife what castle it was and to whom it belonged.

"That is an enchanted castle, and nobody who goes into it ever returns."

But he could not rest, and he was eager to explore the castle. So one morning he ordered his horse to be saddled, and, accompanied by his dog, he rode to the castle. When they reached it they found the gate open. As he went in he saw men and animals all turned to stone. In the hall an old hag was sitting by the fire. When she saw him she pretended to tremble.

"Dear lord," said she, "bind your dog. He might bite me."

He said: "Do not be afraid. He will do you no harm."

He bent down to pat the dog, and at that moment the hag took her wand and struck him with it. He was turned to stone, and his horse and dog too.

The princess waited for her lord, but he did not

return. She mourned for him, and the citizens, who loved their lord, were grieved at his loss.

Now, the other brother looked at his sword, and the sword began to rust; so he was sure that his brother was in trouble. He felt that he must help him, so he rode off in that direction and came to the town. The town was hung with black flags. As he rode through the streets the citizens saw him, and they thought he was their lord, for he had a horse and a dog just like their lord's horse and dog. When the princess saw him, she embraced him and said : "Where have you been so long, my dear husband?"

He said that he had lost his way in the forest and that he had fallen among robbers, and, since he had no choice, he had to pretend to be a robber too, and to promise to stay with them and to show them good hiding-places. The robbers, so he said, admitted him to be of their company, and he had not been able to escape before this.

Everybody was delighted, and the lord's brother was careful enough not to say that he was only the brother. But, whenever they went to bed, he put his sword between himself and the lady. The princess was troubled at this, and she tried to find different explanations for the conduct of her supposed husband. One morning, as he was looking out of the window, he saw that same castle, and he asked what castle it was.

She answered: " I have told you already that it is an enchanted castle, and that nobody who goes there ever returns."

So he thought: " It is surely there that my brother is."

He ordered his horse to be saddled and, without saying a word to anybody, he rode off to the castle. As soon as he entered the castle he saw his brother and his dog turned to stone. He saw, too, all the petrified knights and their horses, and the hag sitting and keeping up the fire.

He said: " You old hag, unless you bring my brother to life again I'll hew you in pieces with this sword of mine."

The hag knew that the sword had magical virtues, and so she said:

" Pray, sir, do not be angry with me. Take that box there and rub the ointment beneath his nose and he will come to life again."

" Curse you, you evil old hag; do it yourself, and instantly."

And he went and caught hold of her wand and struck her with it, and at once she was turned into stone. He had not meant to do that, for he did not know that the wand had such power. He took the box and rubbed the ointment beneath his brother's nose, and the brother came to life again. Then he anointed all the others who had been turned to stone, and they all came to life again. As for the hag, he left her there just as she was.

Then the brothers rode off to the princess. When she saw them, she did not know which of them was her husband, they were so like one another.

So she said: "What am I to do now? Which of you is my lord?"

They came before her and bade her choose the right one. But still she hesitated. So her husband went up to her and took her by the hand and said: "I am the right one and that is my brother."

He told her everything, and she was glad that her real husband had come again. So they lived happily together, and, as for the other brother, he went to seek his fortune elsewhere.

THE WATERNICK

ONCE upon a time there were two children, a boy and a girl. They only had a mother, who was a widow. One day their mother sent them to get some wood for the fire. Off they went. The girl was just learning to knit, so she put a ball of wool in her pocket. They went on as far as they knew the way. Then suddenly they began to wonder whether they could find their way home.

The girl said: "I will bind the end of the thread to a tree, and so we shall be able to find our way back."

So they went on till the thread had all run out. Then they turned back, but they found that wild creatures had broken the thread. What were they to do? They wandered on till night fell, and then they saw that they would have to spend the night in the forest. They came to a pond, and they found that they could not go any farther. So they

walked round the pond till the Waternick got
hold of them. He took them with him, and
there they were.

When he got home with them, his wife was
waiting for him. Round the stove there were
some shelves for vessels that they used for
catching poor souls in. The Waternick and
his wife were delighted with the children; they
decided that they would employ them as servants, so Mrs. Waternick took charge of them.
The children spent some years in this way and
learned about everything under the water.

One day the Waternick went away to catch
some human souls, and he gave orders to Mrs.
Waternick not to leave the children alone.
But the old hag fell asleep, and the children
walked some distance from the hut, till they
thought she would scold them, and so they
returned home. But they meant to go farther
the next day, if only the old hag went to sleep
again. As soon as they were sure that she
was asleep they ran out of the hut and went
as far as they could.

The old hag woke up and cried out: "Where
are you, children?"

She jumped to her feet and ran after them.
They were within a few steps of getting safe

away, when, alas! she overtook them. She took them back and forced them to work, and they had to stay at home besides.

When the Waternick came home, she told him all about it, and the Waternick said · "Never mind, I'll set them to work, and they won't have time to think about making their way home."

So in the morning he took them to the forest and gave them a wooden hatchet and a wooden saw and bade them, fell the trees.

"When they are all cut down, you shall go back again."

So the Waternick left them, and the children began the work at once. They took the saw and tried to cut down a tree. But the saw soon broke and they were done for. So they took the hatchet, and the hatchet split in two after one stroke. They began to cry.

"Things look bad for us," they said.

Since they saw that they could not help themselves, they stayed where they were, and presently they fell asleep. I don't know how long they had been sleeping. But it was already time to go back.

The Waternick came and asked: "Have you finished?"

They said that the hatchet and saw were only made of wood, and that both were broken. He took them home.

Next day the Waternick went about his work, while Mrs. Waternick was busy outside the hut. The children looked at the cups on the shelves. The cups were tilted up. So the girl lifted one of them. And she heard the words: "God speed you!" She lifted another, and the same greeting came again. So she kept on lifting the cups till she had lifted all of them. Human souls had been imprisoned under those cups. Now the hag came into the room and she saw that all the cups had been lifted. She began to curse, and she said that the children would certainly get a good thrashing when the old man came home.

The children often felt lonely; they thought of their mother and wondered if she were still alive, and what they could do to get away. So they decided that the next day, when the hag was sleeping, they would try how far they could get.

"If only we could get as far as home, it would be all right then."

In the morning the girl had to comb Mrs.

Waternick's hair and dress her in her smart dress. When she had finished, Mrs. Waternick had a sleep. Now the children took to their heels; they were as quick as ravens, trying to get away before Mrs. Waternick should wake. Being swift of foot, they reached the shore. They leapt out and ran straight on again. Of course they heard the hag screeching behind them, but they were on dry land, so they thought: "We needn't care for anything now."

The hag soon stopped her pursuit. The children were tired, so they lay down under a tree in the forest and fell asleep. As they were sleeping, somebody woke them up. It was the forester. They told him that they were afraid of falling into the Waternick's hands again. But the forester told them not to be afraid, and asked how they came there. The children told him everything just as it had happened.

Now, the forester remembered that he had heard of a widow who had lost her children. So he thought that these must be the children. He said nothing, but he told his wife to get them some food, and asked the children to sit down and eat. The children thought the food was very nice, so he asked them what they were accustomed to eat. They said they were accustomed to eat flowers. So they ate plenty.

The forester decided to do all he could to get the children home. At last it was discovered where their mother lived, and so the children came back to her, and they lived with her until they died.

THE MAN WHO MET MISERY

ONCE upon a time there lived a rich man, so rich that you might almost say he oozed gold. He had a son, and from his boyhood the lad was a real spendthrift, for he knew nothing about hard times. Yet he had often been told that there was Misery in the world. So when he was grown up, he thought: "Well, I'm sick of staying at home, so I'll go out into the world to see if I can meet Misery."

He told this to his father, and his father said at once: "Yes, you can go. If you stay at home, you'll soon turn into a lazy old woman. You'll get experience in the world, and that can't do you any harm."

So our Francis—that was his name, though really it doesn't matter very much what his name was—took everything he wanted and started off on his travels. So long as he had enough money, he was all right, he couldn't meet with Misery. But when his money was all spent—that's when everybody feels the pinch—he began to hang his head and his travels lost a good deal of their charm. But he told people his name and his father's name, and for a time they helped him. But at last he came into a country that was quite strange to him. There was a vast desert, through which he walked for a long time, and he began to feel hungry and thirsty, but there was no water—no, not so much as would moisten his tongue.

Now, as he went on his way, he saw a flight of stairs going down into a hole, and, without hesitating, down he went.

He came into a cellar, and there he saw a man lying on a table. It was an awfully big man, of the kind that used to be called ogres, and he was snoring like a circular saw.

Francis looked about him, and he saw all sorts of human bones lying about. He thought : "That's a nice mess. I expect the fellow's a man-eater, and he'll swallow me down like a currant. I'm done for now."

He would have liked to go away, but he was afraid to move. But he had a dagger, so he drew it from its sheath without making any noise, and tried to steal up to the ogre quietly. The ogre's head was lying on the table, so he pierced both his eyes with the dagger. The ogre sprang up, cursing horribly. He groped about him and found that he was totally blind.

Francis cleared the stairs in two jumps and off he ran, trying to get as far from the ogre as he could. But the ogre knew the place well and kept close on his heels.

"To think that a shrimp like that could make me suffer so!" he thought; and yet he found that, run as he would, he couldn't catch the lad. So he cried out: "Wait a bit, you worm! Since you're such a champion and have managed to tackle me, I'll give you something to remember me by."

As he said this, he flung a ring at the lad, and the jewel in it shone like flame. The lad heard the ring tinkle as he ran by, so he picked it up and put it on his finger. But as soon as the ring was on his finger, the giant called out: "Where are you, ring?" And the ring answered: "Here I am," and the ogre ran after the sound. Francis jumped on one side, but the ogre called out again, "Where are you?" and the ring answered: "Here!"

So it went on for some time, until Francis was so tired that his only thought was: "Well, if he kills me, he kills me." He tried to pull the ring off, but it clung tight, really cutting into the flesh, and the ogre was still following close on his heels. At last—there was no other choice, for the ring kept on calling out "Here I am"—Francis stretched out that finger, and the ogre broke it off with one grip. Off ran Francis, glad enough to get off with his life.

When he reached home, they asked him : "Did you meet Misery?"

"Indeed I did. I know what it is now. It gave me a nice run for it. It's an awful thing, and there's no joking with it."

NINE AT A BLOW

ONCE upon a time there was a tailor, and, whenever he hadn't a job, he used to spend his time mending stockings. One day after dinner the table was covered with flies. The tailor struck at them with a stocking and killed nine of them at a blow.

As he hadn't any job in hand, he started out to see the world, and his belt had written on it "Nine at a blow." On his way he met a boy, who asked him to buy a finch from him. He bought it, put it in his knapsack, and went on his way. Then he came to a farm where the farmer's wife was making cheese. He asked her for something to eat, so she gave him some sour milk and a piece of Yorkshire cheese. The tailor drank the milk and put the cheese in his knapsack and went on his way. At last he reached a town. It was a hot day, so he lay down and fell asleep. Now, a giant happened to pass that way, and he saw written in golden letters : " Nine at a blow."

So he waked the tailor and asked him : " Have you really killed nine at a blow? "

The tailor answered that he had, and the giant said : " Let's have a trial which of us is the stronger. I'll cast a stone, and it will be an hour before it comes down."

The tailor said : " I'll cast a stone that won't come down at all."

So the giant cast a stone, and it was a full hour before it came down again. Instead of casting a stone, the tailor let the finch go, and, of course, it didn't come back again.

So the giant said : " Let's have another try. I'll crush a stone to powder."

The tailor said : " I'll squeeze water from a stone."

So the giant took a pebble and crushed it to powder. The tailor took the cheese and squeezed it till the water oozed out of it.

The giant gave in, and acknowledged that the tailor was the stronger of the two. So they went on together till they came to a cherry-tree growing near a meadow, and the cherries were ripe. They wanted to pick some of the cherries for themselves. So the tailor climbed the tree, but the giant simply bent down the top of the tree and began to pluck the cherries. When he had finished he let go, and the tailor was flung onto a heap of dry grass piled up in the meadow. So the tailor said: "If it hadn't been for my skill in flying, I should have broken my neck," and he promised to teach the giant how to fly.

So they went on their way again, and they came to a town. The town was all in mourning. They asked the reason, and they were told that a dragon had taken up his headquarters in the church and was killing the people. The king would give a thousand pounds to whoever could kill the dragon. So they told the king that they would kill the dragon.

They ordered a big hammer and a big pair of tongs to be made for them. When they were made, the giant took the tongs and he gave the hammer to the tailor to carry. But the tailor said: "Wouldn't it shame you if people should see us, each carrying such a trifle? Take both the things yourself."

When they came near the church door,

the giant gave the hammer to the tailor, who stuck fast to it. Then the dragon came dashing out, and flung the tailor behind him, but the giant split him in twain. But the tailor protested:

" A nice mess you've made of it. I meant to take the dragon alive. We should have got more money for him so." Then he said: " Now I will teach you how to fly."

So they climbed up the church steeple, and the tailor said: " When I say ' One, two, three,' you must jump." And the giant jumped and broke his neck.

The tailor told the king that the dragon had killed the giant, so he pocketed the thousand pounds for himself.

A CLEVER LASS

ONCE upon a time there was a shepherd. He used to pasture his sheep upon a hill, and one day he saw something glittering on the opposite hill. So he went there to see what it was. It was a golden mortar. He took it up and said to his daughter: " I will give this mortar to our king."

But she said : " Don't do that. If you give him the mortar, you won't have the pestle, and he is sure to ask for it, and then you will get into trouble."

But the shepherd thought that she was only a silly girl. He took the mortar, and, when he came before the king, he said : " Begging your pardon, Mr. King, I want to give you this mortar."

The king answered him roughly : " If you give me the mortar, I must have the pestle as well. Unless the pestle is here within three days; your life will be forfeit."

The shepherd began to lament : "My daughter was right when she said that when you had got the mortar you would want the pestle too. I wouldn't listen to her, so it serves me right."

"Have you such a clever daughter as that?" asked the king.

"Indeed I have," said the shepherd.

"Then tell your daughter that I will marry her, if she comes neither walking nor riding, clothed nor unclothed, neither by day nor by night, neither at noon nor in the morning. And I won't ask for the pestle either."

The shepherd went home and said : "You can get me out of this, if you go to Mr. King neither clothed nor unclothed," and the rest of it.

But the daughter wasn't a bit frightened. She came with the fall of dusk (and that was neither at noon nor in the morning); she dressed herself in fishing-nets ; she took a goat, and she partly rode on the goat and partly she walked.

And when the king saw that she had only a fishing-net on, that she came with the approach of dusk, and that she was partly walking, partly riding on the goat, he was bound to marry her. But he said to her : "You will be my wife so long as you don't give advice to anybody ; but if you do, you must part with me."

Well, she didn't give advice to anybody until one day there was a market in the town, and a farmer's mare had a foal at the market. The foal ran away to another farmer, who was there with a gelding, and the farmer said : "This foal belongs to me."

They went to law about it, and at last the matter came before the king. And the king, considering that every animal ought to run to its mother, decided that a gelding had had a foal.

The farmer who owned the mare went down the stairs, saying over and over again : "The gelding has foaled ! the gelding has foaled !"

The queen heard him, and she said : "Man, you are talking nonsense."

So he told her that he had been at the market, that his mare had foaled, but the foal ran to another farmer who was there with a gelding. "And now," he said, "it has been decided that the gelding has foaled." So he thought there could be no mistake ; at any rate, he couldn't help it.

When the queen heard this story she said: "To-morrow, my lord the king will go out for a stroll. Take a fishing-net, and begin fishing on the road in front of him. The king will ask you: 'Why are you fishing on a dry road?' And you must answer: 'Why not? it's as hopeful as expecting a gelding to foal.' But you must not say who gave you this advice."

So it was. As the king was walking along he saw the farmer fishing on the dry road. He asked him why he was fishing there.

"Why not?" said he, "it's as hopeful as expecting a gelding to foal."

The king at once began to rate the farmer. "That's not out of your own head," he said, and he kept at the farmer until he let the secret out.

So the king came home, summoned the queen, and said to her: "You have been with me for a long time, and you have given advice in spite of all, so you must go to-morrow. But I will allow you to take with you the thing you like best."

It was no good arguing. So the king invited all his courtiers and prepared a splendid banquet. When the banquet was finished, the queen said to the king: "Before we part, you must drink this glass of wine to my health," and she had put some opium into the wine on the sly.

The king drank it at a draught and fell asleep at once. A carriage was got ready, and the queen put the king in it and drove to her father's old hut. There she laid the king on the straw, and, when he woke up, he asked where he was.

"You are with me. Didn't you tell me that I could take the thing I liked best with me?"

The king saw how clever she was, and he said: "Now you can give advice to anybody you like."

And so they drove home again, and he was king and she queen again.

THE SOLDIER AND THE DEVIL

A DISCHARGED soldier was going home. He had only threepence in his pocket. As he was going through a forest he met a beggar. The beggar asked him for a penny. The soldier gave him one, and went on his way. Then he met another beggar. This beggar was very ill, and he asked the soldier for a penny. So the soldier gave him the other penny. Then he met a third beggar. This beggar was half-dead. The soldier took pity on him and gave him the third penny. Soon after he had left the forest our Lord appeared to him, and in return for those three pennies He granted him three boons. For the first boon the soldier chose a pipe that should be full of tobacco whenever he wished, so that he might always have a smoke handy. The second boon he asked was that, if he wanted to put any one in his knapsack, they should be in it as soon as he said : " Leap into that knapsack." The third boon was that his purse should be full of gold coins whenever he knocked on it.

Our Lord said : "So be it!"

Soon afterwards he came to a mill and asked for a night's lodging. They said that they only had one room for themselves ; the other one was haunted by a devil every midnight. But the soldier wasn't afraid. He said that they could leave him there alone ; he didn't mind a bit.

He sat down at the table and played cards. When midnight came there was a terrible noise, and the devil appeared, sure enough. When he saw the soldier playing cards he grinned ; he was sure he had him. So he sat down opposite him and began to play too. It was nearly one o'clock at last, time for him to go, so he caught hold of the soldier and tried to tear him in pieces. But he had no success. For the soldier said : " Leap into my knapsack," and the devil was in it. Then the soldier threw the sack with the devil in it under the bed, and went to sleep in the bed.

In the morning, as soon as he had got up, the millers went to see if the soldier was still alive. They were greatly surprised to find him all right. They said they would give him anything he wanted, but he wouldn't take anything. Off he went, and called at a blacksmith's. He told the blacksmith to give the devil in the sack a good hammering, and then he let the devil go.

After that he came into a town. He heard that there was a count's daughter there who was an accomplished cardplayer. She won everybody's money from them. He went to her palace and asked her if she would play with him. She was ready. So they played and played, but she couldn't win all his money from him, for his purse was always fuller than before. It was late by now and the lady was sick of the game, so he went to bed. He put the three precious gifts on the table, but when he got up in the morning they were gone; the lady had stolen them from him. He grieved over his bad luck, but it was no use, and he had to leave the palace.

As he went on his way, he saw a fine apple-tree by the side of the road with delicious apples on it. So he took an apple and ate half of it. Then he went on his

way, but he was surprised to see that everybody who looked at him ran away from him.
So he went to a well and saw that he had
horns on his head; that came from his eating
the apple. Back he went, and he found a
pear-tree; he ate half of a pear and the horns
fell off.

He thought that he would give the other
half of the apple to the lady, and perhaps
she would get horns too. So he went and
gave her the half apple. She enjoyed it very
well, but soon horns grew on her head. The
count called together all the doctors and
asked them to operate on the horns. But
the more they cut at the horns the longer
they grew. So the king proclaimed that she
would marry the man who should rid her of
the horns, but if he failed, his life should be
forfeit. So the soldier came back and told
the lady that he would rid her of the horns
if she would give him his three treasures
back. She agreed at once. So he gave her
the other half of the pear; she ate it, and
the horns fell off.

The soldier was quite happy now. One
day he met Death, and he said to
him: " Leap into my knapsack." And

Death was immediately imprisoned in the knapsack.

The soldier was carrying Death about for some time, until at last the Lord appeared to him and told him he must not do that: he must let Death go, for people could not die, and there would soon be too many of them in the world. So he let Death go. He wanted to go to Heaven himself. But he went to Hell, and as he drew near Hell the devils closed the gate, they were so frightened of him. When he reached the gate of Heaven, he knocked. St. Peter opened the gate, but he wouldn't let him in. The soldier asked him to let him have just one peep, so that at least he might know what Heaven looked like.

Now, he remembered that he still had his soldier's cloak in his knapsack, so he took it out of the knapsack and threw it into Heaven. Then he jumped after it and sat down on it, and then he said he was sitting on his own property. He sat there for a full hundred years, though it only seemed a short time to him. But he couldn't come to an agreement with St. Peter on the case, so our Lord told him that he must first die, for no living people were admitted into Heaven. So the soldier had to leave the premises. He returned to this world, and afterwards he went to Heaven again, and there he is still, as right as rain.

176

177

OLD NICK AND KITTY

ONCE upon a time there was an old maid-servant on a farm. She was a score or two years old, but she wanted to get married, though nobody would even touch her. She never missed a dance : she was sure to turn up at every one of them, though nobody ever asked her to dance. So at last she said :

" l'd dance with Old Nick if only he'd come."

The clock struck eleven and a youth clothed in green entered the room. He went straight up to our Kitty and began to dance with her. All the girls couldn't keep from laughing, but they daren't laugh openly. So they held their aprons over their faces. Kitty was very angry, but she kept on dancing like the wind. She thought : " Let the fools laugh ; they'd be glad enough to dance with the lad themselves."

It was hard upon twelve now, and Old Nick—for Old Nick it was—had to start

for home. But Kitty wouldn't let him go.
What was he to do with her? He was
absolutely at a loss what to do, for she was
clinging on to him behind.

He went to the pond, thinking he'd be
able to throw her in. He tried to do it, but
she clasped him round the neck and he
couldn't manage it. So off he went to Hell
with her. But the people of Hell made
an outcry against her and wouldn't let her
stay at any price.

"Hang it all!" says Old Nick, "I can't
go all round the world with her."

At last he met a shepherd: "I say, shepherd," says he, "would you like this maiden
here?"

"A nice maiden that is, the ugly old
spinster! Keep her for yourself. You can
pickle her."

Now, when the devil saw that he was going
to fail again, he promised the shepherd a
heap of money, only to rid himself of the
hideous old crone. But the shepherd refused.

"I'll make it so much," says Old Nick. .

"Well, if you will, I agree."

Now, the shepherd was a good-looking
fellow, and Kitty was easily persuaded to stay

with him. He had lots of money now, and he had the same idea as the devil, to throw her into the pond. What else could he do with such a hideous old hag? He had a great fur coat, and he put it on so high over his head that she couldn't catch hold of his neck, and, plump! off she went into the pond. But, you know, a bad one's a bad one, and you can't get rid of them so easily. So it was with Kitty. She wasn't drowned.

A short time after this, Old Nick had an appointment with a man. I don't exactly know how the case stood, but anyhow the devil was to get him. The man asked the shepherd to save him; he was quite ready to pay him well for it.

"All right," says the shepherd, "I can do that much for you. Old Nick and I are the best of friends."

Now, a crowd of people had collected and they were all wondering how it was going to end. In comes Old Nick. The shepherd runs to meet him and: "Old Kitty's here asking for you," says he.

The devil left things as they were, and before you could say "Jack Robinson" he was off. So it all turned out all right.

THE KNIGHT BAMBUS

THERE was a poor gamekeeper once, who had suffered from hard times all his life, so as he grew older, he wanted to get rich. He was only an under-forester. One day the forester said : " Near those old ruins, you know the ones I mean, a fox or a roe, or some creature of that sort, often crosses my path, and I can never manage to hit it, though I have shot at it a hundred times. If you happen to be going in that direction, look out for it."

When the gamekeeper heard this, the first thing he did was to go to the ruins. Just as he got there, a huge fox appeared with a rustling noise. The gamekeeper felt uneasy, but the fox disappeared at once, so he sat down, put five big charges in his gun, and waited. It wasn't long till the fox appeared again, and this time he was carrying a young fawn in his mouth. The gamekeeper shot at him—boom ! The fox cried out, and ran

off into the bushes.   But the gamekeeper saw
that the fawn had run away and hidden itself
in a cave.   He thought : "The fox cried out,
so he has some of my shots in his fur coat.
I'll get him some other time."

So he went into the ruins through the gate.
Within, there was a courtyard all deserted,
and with its wall fallen down.   So the gamekeeper passed through the courtyard and came
into a spacious cellar.   There he saw three
lamps burning, and looking round, he was
filled with amazement.   But all this was as
nothing, for in the corner were three glittering
heaps of golden coins and one heap of big
gold pieces.   The gamekeeper reflected: " If
I had all that, I should give up gamekeeping
and have a splendid time."

No sooner had he said this than a grey
old man appeared and asked : " What are you
looking for, gamekeeper? "

" Well, I shot at a fox and he ran in somewhere here, and so I'm wandering about
looking for him."

" You won't get the fox you're looking for,
for I am he."

" And why are you here in a fox's shape?
What's the reason of that ? "

" I am the Knight Bambus, and all these forests belong to this castle. I was a robber-knight, and so as a punishment I have to keep watch here now."

" And how long is it to last ? "

" When three poor people come here, and each of them takes away two sackfuls of gold, I shall be delivered. I am bound to give all this gold away for nothing. Already I have outlived three generations of my kinsmen here."

Then he bade him fetch two leather sacks from the other room and collect the gold into them, filling them up to the brim. He must keep it all for himself and must not tell any one what he had seen. The gamekeeper promised that he wouldn't even tell his wife, Háticka, how he had got the money. So he filled the two sacks up to the brim, and the old man helped him to hoist them on to his shoulders and saw him out of the door. All the time he kept warning him to keep his mouth shut : " For what a woman knows all the world knows ; that's gospel truth, sure enough."

So the gamekeeper left the castle, carrying those two sacks, and the man shook hands with him before he left. At the border of the forest, near a beech-tree, his wife, Háta, was standing looking for him. She ran up to him.

"Great Heavens, Florian! where have you been all this long time? I have been looking everywhere for you for three days."

Now Florian was delighted that his wife had come to meet him, so he blurted out: "Háticka, wife, Count Bambus has given me these two sacks of gold pieces. Have a look here—see what heaps of the stuff there are!" and he let one of the sacks fall on the ground. But behold! instead of gold there were only rustling leaves in it. Then he remembered that he was not to say anything about it. He frowned, and his wife burst into tears; and they had to spend the rest of their life, until they died, in poverty just as before.

FRANCIS AND MARTIN

ONCE there was a father who had only one son, Francis by name. They had a farmhand called Martin. One day Martin and Francis were ploughing behind the barn. Francis's mother brought their meal for them, and Francis said: "Well, mother, the old man must have a lot more money than he lets on to have. We are not in debt, and yet he's always complaining that he hasn't any money."

"Well, my son, you see, he's built that large building."

Next day Francis and Martin were ploughing together again. They decided that they must get on the old man's track to see whether he had any money, and where he hid it. Francis promised Martin that, if he could find it out, he would build a cottage for him at the back of the barn. So they agreed that Martin should stay away from church to try to find out if the farmer had any money hidden away at home.

When Sunday came, Francis went to church, but Martin kept on saying he wouldn't go, until the farmer forced him to go. So he dressed for church and went out through the farm gate. But he came back on the other side, climbed over the fence, and hid himself in the barn. Soon after this the farmer came into the barn, carrying a basket full of coins. He dug a hole in the threshing-floor, put the money in it, and said: " Black Barabbas! preserve this money for me! Thou black bird! I put it in thy power!" Then he went and fetched a second basket and put it in the hole. But while he was gone to fetch the money, Martin slipped out of his hiding-place, took some of the money, and put it in his boots. Now, the farmer came back again with a third basket, and said once more: " Thou black bird! keep this money for me, and let nobody else have it, unless he gets it by ploughing this threshing-floor with three black goats!"

As he was saying these words, a blackbird was soaring above his head and crying out: " Master, what about the money in the boots?"

But the farmer did not understand what it

meant, and so he went to look at his own boots, which were in the room. But he found no money there, so he was angry and said: " What, you devil! it's rubbish you are talking. I've looked in my boots and there's nothing there." Then he buried the money, stamped down the threshing-floor hard again, and went out.

Martin went to the stable, and there he found Francis waiting for him to tell him what the parson's sermon had been about that day, so that he would know what to say if the farmer asked him about it.

Soon afterwards the old man was taken ill and died. The two lads were pleased at this, for they hoped that they wouldn't be long about getting the money. Martin got three black goats, he put them in the plough, and sent Francis to plough there. The wind began to blow violently, and the whole barn looked as though it were on fire. He was frightened and stopped ploughing, and immediately the whole barn was just as it had been before. So he went out of the barn and asked Martin to plough for him. Martin started, and, although the wind blew violently enough, he kept on ploughing until he got the money.

When Francis had the money, he began to build just as he wanted until he had spent it all. Then he gave Martin the sack.

Martin said sorrowfully: "This is the world's gratitude."

WITCHES AT THE CROSS

THOUGH the witches used to be pretty lively in other places, they were fond of climbing up and down the cross that stands by the road to Malá Čermá (near Slaný). Joe Hilma heard tell of this, so he took his horse and off he rode to see. He took with him a piece of chalk which had been blessed, and made a circle with it. Then he went into the circle and waited till midnight. Then, sure enough, he saw the witches, a great swarm of them, climbing up and down the cross. They didn't see him while this was going on, but when he rode out of the circle, off went the witches after him. He galloped home at full speed. When he rode into the yard they were close on his heels. They couldn't go any farther, for they had no power to do it. I don't know how it happened, but one of them flung a burning broom after him. The broom hit the door, and the door was burned. Joe had quite enough of seeing the witches.

THE WITCH AND THE HORSESHOES

ONCE there was a farmer's wife—I can't tell you which one—who was a witch. Now these folks used to have a feast every Eve of St. Philip and St. James. As soon as they began to burn the brooms she couldn't rest: go she must. So she stripped her clothes off, and, standing under the chimney, she anointed herself with some ointment. When she had finished, she said: " Fly, but don't touch anything." And away she flew in the twinkling of an eye. Yes, that was just how it was.

But the farmhand was watching all this from the stables, and he watched carefully where she put the ointment. So he went in too, stripped his clothes off, and anointed himself. He said: " Fly, but don't touch anything." And off he flew till he came to the place where the witches were having their feast. Now, when he came there, the farmer's wife knew him, and, to hide herself from him, she turned herself into a white horse. But he did not lose sight of the horse. He mounted it and went to the smith with it, and told him to shoe it. Next day the woman had four horseshoes on, two on her hands and two on her feet. And she had to stay like that always!

193

THE HAUNTED MILL

THERE was a haunted mill, and, dear me, what was it like! A rope-dancer came there with some monkeys. In the evening the Water-nick came with a basketful of fishes. He made a fire and fried the fishes. Meanwhile the monkeys had been sitting behind the stove, but when the Nick put the fishes in the pan and was tasting whether they were done, the monkeys came from behind the stove, and one of them put its paw into the pan. The man smacked him over the paw and said: " Get away, pussy ! You didn't catch them, so don't eat them." And the monkey ran away.

After awhile comes another monkey and puts his paw in the pan. He smacked him too and said the same. But the rope-dancer had a bear, too, which was lying under the table all the time; and, when he heard the Waternick speak, he came from under the table, ran straight to the pan, and put his paw into it. The Waternick did the same to him as he had done to the monkeys. But the bear couldn't stand that. He sprang upon the poor Waternick and gave him a good beating. The Waternick had to run off, leaving the fishes behind. He didn't haunt the mill any more, and that's how they got rid of him.

CPSIA information can be obtained
at www.ICGtesting.com
Printed in the USA
FSOW02n1141050118
43099FS